STRANGER
THAN FICTION

STRANGER THAN FICTION

X H A N T I

STRANGER THAN FICTION

iUniverse books may be ordered through booksellers or by contacting:

iUniverse
1663 Liberty Drive
Bloomington, IN 47403
www.iuniverse.com
844-349-9409

ISBN: 978-1-6632-3435-3 (sc)
ISBN: 978-1-6632-3436-0 (e)

Library of Congress Control Number: 2022900388

Print information available on the last page.

iUniverse rev. date: 01/04/2022

THE ESCAPE

I vaguely remember clearing security. The airport was noisy, busy, bustling, as usual, but I barely noticed, just as I was barely aware of all the many details of handing over documents, passport, ticket; answering questions; and jumping through all the many hoops that are part of airline travel these days.

But I do remember standing on the other side of the security checkpoint at Miami International, so weak with relief that my legs could barely hold me up. I knew I was breathing, but I couldn't feel the rise and fall of my chest. I knew my heart was beating—it had to be—but it felt as though the steadfast, rhythmic organ that was keeping me alive had been replaced by something savage and wild that couldn't be contained.

I'd done it. After years of suffering and months of plotting and planning, I'd escaped from Storm without a scratch, still hanging on to everything I'd entered into our marriage with: my possessions, my dignity, and my sanity.

Morning light streamed through the rows of glass panes above. It was getting late, and I knew I should be heading to my gate. But I couldn't. Not yet.

Harried travelers brushed past, and I realized that I was still standing in everyone's way. I took several steps backward, dragging my carry-on bag with me. In spite of the ruckus, the chatter, and the muffled announcements from the speakers overhead, I could hear the *clack-clack* of my heels on the tiles.

Then, as though a passing angel had reached out and caressed my cheek, all my anxiety and nervousness rolled away, replaced by an indescribable calm.

I would never have to see my husband again.

RULE 1: DRAW ON
YOUR LEGACY

I am descended from a long line of wretches, at least as far as the men go. Those that fell from the uppermost branches of my family tree valued their masculinity highly—and their definition of masculinity involved screwing around with as many women as they could, as often as they could.

They chased skirt tails in the same way puppies chase chickens, with scant regard for the feelings of their wives or partners. They reproduced as though trying to repopulate a postapocalyptic world. They mixed and mingled with women of every stripe, blind to race, religion, or origin, resulting in the large and variegated broods that peopled my youth.

On paper this sounds quite horrifying, but I know I'm not alone. Rare is the woman who cannot testify to the wayward and indiscriminate tendencies of our men.

My father's endless pursuit of women hurt my mother, frayed his marriage, and sent ripples of discord through our family.

In my teens, this was difficult for me to understand. I guess, as most young girls do, I looked up to him, the first man in my life. For a long time, I puzzled over why he would do this and why he seemed unable to rein in his own desires in the face of mounting evidence of the damage he was doing to his family. Later in life, I surmised that it was less a matter of pursuing pleasure and more one of a burning need to feed his low self-esteem.

I won't bore you by making pronouncements about a Napoleon complex; I'm not even convinced that's actually a thing. But my dad was very short. He was insecure about this, and to make it worse, he never thought of himself as good looking. When I look at old photographs of him as a youngster, even the ones we used on the program for his funeral, I find him quite attractive. But he never saw himself as such.

A nagging sense of unfulfillment probably fed the monster. His father died when he was very young, and he grew up with a stepmother who had a mental illness. He graduated at the top of his class with the desire to become an attorney, but his folks couldn't afford it. They sent him to work in a more lucrative trade industry instead. And although he worked there until his retirement, it was always his greatest regret.

He would have made an outstanding attorney and did well in his chosen career; he was the kind of man who insisted on doing whatever he did well. But there was always that little something missing in his life; his candle was sputtering out, and he desperately sought ways to keep it alight.

Both my maternal and paternal grandfathers were just as bad when it came to having affairs and chasing tail, even though they made the effort to raise their children—my parents, aunts, and uncles—very circumspectly.

My mother's dad, Leonard Gordon, was a tall, stately man; he had to bend to come through doorways. He was originally from the Caribbean. He'd wear a white suit every Monday when he made his pilgrimage to the local hospital to get his insulin, and he always, always sported a hat and cane. Sporty, right?

And yet he had no professional ambition. I never got the feeling he was aware of his true potential—or maybe he was but didn't care to achieve it. He lived in low income housing on for years, where the rent was just fifteen dollars a month. He made fairly good money and held down a stable job. Yet it never occurred to him to buy himself a piece of land. Land was so cheap then, but no …

When it came to the ladies, he was someone different. My grandfather was a player. He was screwing with my grandmother but refused to marry her, because she was jet black and he was high yellow. You know how it was back then … well, how it still is, to some extent.

My grandmother bore him two girls, and each one took after one parent. My mother got his height and coloring, and her sister, my aunt, was short and dark like granny. They both had Coke-bottle figures, which my mother insists I have, although I tell her, with no trace of false modesty, that I've never noticed that. Hard to look at yourself like that, isn't it?

Anyway, he lived with another woman after my grandmother moved on and got married, taking my mom with her. My grandmother then had another child, giving me an uncle who is thirteen years younger than my mom.

My grandmother was one of—wait for it—the twenty-two children that her father had with two women. She was lucky number thirteen. They were interspersed; in other words, great-grandfather was romancing them, even a husband of sorts to both of them, at the same time. They all lived together—one big roiling, tumbling family.

To this day, I have no idea which of my great aunts and uncles belonged to which woman; I just grew up knowing they were all my grandmother's brothers and sisters.

My grandmother, to her credit, refused to be married off at a tender age like her other sisters; she ran away, and took up residence in another town to make sure that didn't happen—which was likely, given how overbearing her father was. Years later, as he began losing his eyesight, but gaining a realization that his sons were stealing his money, he hired a taxi for the day, found my grandmother, and sweet-talked her into coming back to live with and care for him. This caused more family conflict, because it was only when he died that it became common knowledge that he'd left all his land and property in her care. While it belonged to all of his children, nobody wanted to spend the money to divide it up. She'd also inherited her own separate piece, which my siblings and I inherited. I'm hoping that the larger piece will be inherited by the generation below me, my daughter and her cousins, because it's important for us to ensure that the next generation has a starting advantage in an uneven playing field.

My great-grandfather was verbally, but not physically, abusive, to both of his wives. At one point, he discovered one of his belts was missing. It turned out that my aunt, child number twenty-two, had been the culprit; she cut it to pieces in a fit of anger and buried it. But he blamed his wife, my great-grandmother; and the argument that followed became legendary. It was the tipping point for her, and she left.

She survived by doing odd jobs. On her day off, she used to visit my grandmother, her daughter, until she eventually moved in with them. She'd only been with them for a short time when, one day, she had a quarrel with my grandmother's husband, who wasn't my grandfather (yes, I know, it's complicated). Undaunted, she rolled up her mattress, balanced it on her head, and walked ten miles to her sister's house. She then moved to the mountains, specifically sparsely populated area which was undeniably, a bold move for a single woman. Eventually Great-Grandmother Jane Greaves saved up enough money and built a one-room house, where she squatted on wild, undeveloped land, without neighbors. My mother remembers traveling for hours by public transportation with my grandmother and my aunt, dropping off at the bottom of the mountain, and walking up the hill through the densely forested areas to visit her. A single woman, living alone, more than seventy years ago. I think I have her blood flowing in my veins!

So at the time of the argument with my great-grandmother, my grandmother's husband sold himself as a natural healer, and people came to him for both physical and spiritual healing. The story goes that a woman turned up one afternoon seeking help—or at least pretending to. It soon came to light that this was my step-grandfather's bit of skirt on the side, and the woman had no shame in moving into my grandmother's house and making herself at home.

When my four-foot-seven grandmother dared to complain, that six-foot, three-hundred-pounder of a man grabbed my grandmother, all ninety-five pounds of her, and shoved her face into the fireside. There was little she could do or say, but she took the course of action many oppressed West Indian women before her had. That night while he was sleeping, she boiled a pot of oil and straddled his sleeping form, holding the pot in one hand, fresh and fragrant from the stove.

He opened his eyes with a start and looked up into the face of a woman who meant business. "Lay your hand on me again," she promised, "and you will not survive the oil."

And he believed her. He tells the story that for two weeks he couldn't sleep, and thereafter he stayed his hand.

To understand my grandmother it's important to understand her history. My great-grandfather died at 109; I guess he's taking a well-deserved rest. That age wasn't unusual for us; we're a long-lived bunch. All of my grandmother's siblings except for baby number twenty-two died in their nineties or more. One even died at 103. My grandmother died at 92, and even up to a few years before her passing she was caring for two of her siblings, aged 97 and 98.

My paternal grandfather migrated from yet another Caribbean island with his two brothers. He, too held a steady and well respected job. One of his brothers had settled in the very mountain side my great grandmother had moved to and the other, as we're now being told, moved to one of the smaller islands. My grandfather had four children, only two of whom had the same mother. There was only one girl in the bunch. He died when my father was young, leaving him to care for a mentally ill mother.

The men made a mess of my family, leaving it as tangled and knotted as an unraveled ball of twine. Children growing up in such a family often inherit a legacy of chaos—a loud, discordant clanging that echoes through their own marriages.

But I feel that my legacy was not one of confusion but rather one of strength, passed on to me by the many strong women in my bloodline: my mother, grandmothers, and great-grandmothers, who were sent reeling time and again by their circumstances but who got to their feet each and every time they were knocked down.

This strength they passed on to me is probably the most important thing I have ever inherited, and in turn, I have passed it on to my only child, my daughter. I made sure she understands two things: (1) that she must never depend on a man, ever, no matter how much she loves him, and (2) that she must never, ever, settle, because her mother settled one time too many, and it almost cost her her life.

A GIRLHOOD HAPPY
AND SAFE

I was born in in a small town. My brother followed two years later, and in another two years, my sister turned up.

We lived in a happy little cul-de-sac where the matriarchal family, after whom it was named, held court at the end of the street in a huge house. They were benefactors of sorts, making sure the other families lining the street were okay.

They owned their property, while the rest of us were renting. We and the other kids were always swarming over there to play in their yard, but they never seemed to mind. They had four kids of their own, the last of whom was disabled, so I guess they understood.

They never acted as though they were better than anyone else. When a friend of the matriarch, started her dance company, she made sure all the little girls got to dance. She was a sweetheart.

We rented an upstairs apartment with three bedrooms. My mom converted one into her sewing room, and we kids slept in one. As the eldest, I had my own bed, while the other two shared a double-decker.

The family, who lived downstairs, had eight boys, so you can imagine the chaos. Then there was the another family of eight across the road, who were originally from Curaçao. Their father crafted tortoiseshell jewelry for a living. Today one of the eight boys is a homeless drug addict living on the streets. My mother gives him food whenever she sees him.

We always had a car; maybe that's where my love of driving came from. Our first car was a PG series, which, as you can guess, takes us back to the 1950s.

I attended "private school"—really kindergarten—while we lived in that little cul de sac. I can remember my mother walking me over to school every day. I was dressed all in brown, from my hair ribbons down to my tall socks. I went there from the age of two, and when I was four, a year younger that the average, I began attending grade school. At age six I skipped a year and matriculated to high school a year younger than my cohort.

I remember causing quite a ruckus when I selected an outlier as my first choice of high schools. My teacher was not happy with this. She called Daddy in to her office and directed him to make me change my selection to St. Joseph's Convent as my first choice instead. Fortunately for me, Daddy didn't budge. His reaction was "It's her choice." He did, however, query my choice, to which I responded that the convent focused too much on academics and I wanted to have a more well-rounded education. I know, I know—a very profound statement for one so young. And I did enjoy a well-rounded education. I participated in every sport, sang, played the flute, and danced. While at primary school, my siblings and I walked to school together every day. By the time I was eleven and had been attending high school for three months, my parents had purchased land and built a house, and we moved to the suburbs. The process of getting to school changed. If Daddy was on day shift, he'd drop us off. If not, we took public transportation and then walked to our grandmother's house for lunch.

As many women did at the time, my mother was a stay-at-home mom for most of her life, but that didn't mean she let her skills lie fallow. Mummy had endless energy and a tremendous sense of style. She divided her time between homemaking, caring for us three—well, four, if you count my father—and dressmaking.

She constantly searched fashion books and magazines to see what was trending in Europe and the United States, and this knowledge made her extremely popular with the fashionable ladies of the town. She made wedding dresses for the mayor's daughters, and could sew anything from confirmation dresses for young ladies to gorgeous evening gowns for New Year's Eve balls. The folks in the energy sector were well known for their parties, and when those happened, stylish women knew to come to her if they wanted to make a stylishly elegant entrance.

If most skills and talents are handed down from generation to generation, it's obvious that no one told my mother, because while she certainly gave me her sense of style and love of looking good, she neglected to pass on whatever DNA is required to excel in the domestic arts. I do not sew. I cannot sew—except, perhaps, for a spot of quick hem repair—and I am not interested in learning. There are way too many exceptional designers out there for me to worry about ever going out of style, so I'd rather not put my ineptitude with a needle to the test. While I'm on the subject, I also do not cook. I can scramble a few eggs, of course, and boil rice, if I'm so inclined, but the prospect of converting a heap of loosely related ingredients into a culinary masterpiece is so foreign to me that it might as well be sorcery. I'll dine out or take out, thank you. And of course, my mother's kitchen door is always wide open.

You might wonder how a household with three children could function with one child, the eldest female at that, treating the kitchen like the Badlands, but surprisingly, my parents were okay with that. My sister took to the kitchen like a natural, picking up quite a bit of my slack in the process. For this I am grateful. My sister would be the first to admit that it was good training, and almost a harbinger of what was to come for her in later life, as she eventually opened her own restaurant. And do I feel guilty? Nope. Not even a little bit.

So, as old-fashioned as they were, my family didn't banish their firstborn girl-child to the kitchen. Instead they identified a talent in me and did everything they could to nurture it. That talent was, and still is, my academic strength. My father recognized it early on and decided it should be my focus. When he traveled, which he did quite frequently, he brought toys for the others, but he'd always bring me a book, to my absolute delight.

My love for books consumed me and eclipsed all else. When I wasn't reading, I was thinking of reading. I got to the point of reading three books in one weekend. *Don't call me to do dishes. Don't call me to watch you cook. Don't call me to clean anything. Don't even call me to eat. I'm reading!*

I read anything and everything: biology, Greek mythology, Shakespeare. I used to get CliffsNotes guides for famous novels and read those. I think it was my early interest in mythology that influenced my fascination with Egyptian culture, which eventually became a commonality between me and Storm.

If I had nothing else to read, I'd resort to short novels: Mills & Boon, that kind of thing. But once I had something new, I got fixated. I didn't want to do anything else. I'd chain-read books in the same way some people chain-smoke cigarettes. In fact, my current reading prescription has one of my eyes worse than the other, and I have only my addiction to blame for that. At night, after my parents called lights out, I'd lie on my side, meaning one eye was typically under the covers, and read with a flashlight.

All that reading stood me in good stead when it came to exams. I ended up earning graduating top of my class. My brother was not so lucky the first time but redeemed himself the second time. I guess the fear of disappointing my parents a second time was enough to get him to buckle down.

My sister, on the other hand, did not do as well. For a long time, she resented my brother and me for our academic prowess— especially me. Books weren't really her thing; where she excelled was in the kitchen. She used to say, "Between the two of you, you excel academically, but neither of you can boil water!"

She gleefully threw that fact in our faces whenever we fought— or, at least, whenever she and my brother fought, because they were at it a lot. It even got physical once or twice, and she usually got the upper hand.

We still look back at that and laugh. "I could never even get a blow in," my brother still says. "She would come at me like a windmill!"

You know those families you can hear shouting at each other in the street, who fight and hug and make up and fight again, and who air their dirty laundry whenever and wherever, never mind who saw or heard? That wasn't us. We weren't very expressive, and we seldom let our emotions get out of hand. And my mother was big on keeping up appearances and always walked with her head held high even in her awareness that everyone knew my father was a whore.

As a child, I did not judge my family, with all their many marriages, infidelities, and children born inside and outside of relationships. They were simply my family, large and energetic and overflowing with humanity.

As an adult, I look back on it as dysfunctional. Growing up within my parents' seemingly emotionless marriage could have had a detrimental effect on my own view of love, but it didn't. This is probably due in part to my love of books, including Mills & Boons and the like. These book-perfect romances were sharply juxtaposed with my reality, and this is what let me hold on to my ideals. I have always been and will always be a die-hard romantic. I still believe in my knight in shining armor.

My parents' marriage was a partnership, if not a romance. It was a business deal in which the end product was their children. For a while, my father kept up with his investment. He'd come home and they'd split up the money: "This is for food. This is for the fridge payment." He stumped up the cash for necessities: utilities, mortgage, and the like. My mom paid for everything else—the niceties: a guitar for my brother, a car for me. When my father wasn't giving us money, he would help himself to my mother's. My grandmother soon found a way to thwart him, presenting herself at the house every Friday evening when people came to pay for and collect the fancy clothes my mother had made for them, and standing at the door, collecting the cash. My mother never complained. She knew that if my grandmother didn't assume collection duties, my father would.

We lived very frugally. We had everything we needed, though not necessarily everything we *wanted*. Our clothes were clean and were always matching. With her sense of style, my mom would have hives if one of her children left the house in any getup that reflected badly on her. Our hair was always combed, and we never stepped outside without slippers on.

That first year when we moved to the suburbs, money was so tight that my parents convinced us that the house itself was our Christmas present. We were so excited! It was the perfect con job.

We desperately wanted a bike, but my parents could afford only one for the three of us to share, and this they presented to us the next Christmas. We were delighted! There was absolutely no whining or complaining about having to take turns. It was even too small, but we rode it anyway, through the cane fields, one by one. We never did anything unless we three did it together. That was our parents' standing rule.

Despite how careful my parents always were with money—or perhaps because of it—we always had a car. Sundays were a big thing for us. On Sundays, we did the family thing. More often than not, we went to the beach. And of course there would be all-out war with two back windows and three children. So we devised all manner of ways in which to arbitrate over who sat where, from the tried-and-true method of "first to call dibs gets it" to jostling and wrestling, to earnestly searching for divine signs. We would count the number of oil pumps we passed in the oil fields; whoever counted the most on the way out would get a window seat on the way back. I wouldn't want to say there was cheating, but ... there was probably cheating.

My mom never did anything by half-measures, so as you can imagine, these Sunday afternoon junkets were a *grand zaffaire*. She'd always pack a sumptuous Sunday picnic lunch, which we'd share as a family, notwithsanding the fact that we were on the beach, surrounded by sand. Then, before we went swimming, my father would bend forward, touch the water with his fingertips, and make the sign of the cross. Then we skipped happily in, knowing we were protected. The same routine was carried out not once, not twice, but every single time.

Other than the regular beach "lime", or the occasional dance recital, on the weekends we didn't venture out, we'd gather around the table for a big Sunday lunch. My father would always talk politics. It was important to him. He expected me, especially, as the eldest, to follow what he was saying and join in the discussion. He was very good about predicting what would happen in the political era.

He was passionate about what he believed in, well read, and very eloquent. He was president of the labor union for his company and led the salary for many, many years. He was on the board of several credit unions. There was even talk that he could have become prime minister one day, had he had the drive and the desire to work toward it; and had he not let his love of women damage his reputation and decision-making to such an extent, he might have achieved that goal.

He was a brilliant man, just brilliant, but he had one weakness: women. His roving eye and his never-ending quest for one more conquest was his downfall. He started one of his many affairs when I was three months old. Most of his women were just passing fancies, but there were three in his lifetime with whom he stayed over an extended period.

Honestly, despite my father's infidelities, I thought of my parents' marriage as a good one, at least until I was in my mid-teens. I never saw my father raise his voice to my mother—not one time. Certainly he never raised his hand. This doesn't mean he didn't have his faults—and almost all of those faults were female. It also didn't mean that he wasn't manipulative and didn't engage in mental abuse. Of course, my mother and I, in our current enlightened state, can only now identify his behavior as such.

When I was just about seventeen, my father turned up at home with a little boy in tow and announced that this was his son. As children, we didn't understand the implications of the arrival of this infant interloper. Nor did we care, quite frankly. We never understood the repercussions and connotations that came with an outside child. In hindsight, and with the clarity of maturity, I can only imagine the impact it must have had on my mother's life. It must have been like a depth charge going off. I know that affairs and extramarital children were quite the norm in those days, and in many ways they still are. But the human price, in terms of pain and heartache, is still a terrible one to ask anybody to pay.

Sometimes I wonder whether—and even pray that—my mother was numb in the wake of my father's many infidelities so that this baby's arrival didn't completely devastate her. To be brutally honest, we're a bit surprised and rather relieved that there weren't more than this one and the one other (still being challenged) that appeared some twenty years later. My father's arrogance must have trickled down to his may consorts—yes, down, because, in hindsight it is plain that they were always lesser than he was either in stature (many were waitresses) or in age (as in the case of the daughter of his then best friend). I speak of the arrogance trickling down because, incredibly, there was one occasion when this baby brother's mother called up Mummy and asked her to meet her in Skinner Park, whereupon she began whining about how my father—get this—was horning her (outside woman number one) with yet another woman (outside woman number two). My mother listened with a half-smile playing on her lips and answered in her usually contained and classy tone, "Sounds like a personal problem to me!" She then sailed off. That's the kind of woman who raised me.

Years later, when my baby brother was an adult, he went to visit my mother in New York to apologize. By then he was privy to some truths concerning the circumstances of his birth, and he rightly deduced that his existence had come with a price: an innocent woman's marriage. He even noted that our father's affair with his mother was not the passionate illicit romance many of us imagine extramarital affairs to be, with breathless clandestine meetings between two people who just can't stay away from each other. It was a lot more cold-blooded than that.

For his mother, my father was the outside man—an addendum to her own primary relationship. She was sleeping with a policeman who coincidentally and conveniently shared my father's name. She was only *reasonably* certain that her last daughter was the policeman's and not my father's.

Worse yet, the relationship was based more on economics than passion. When my baby brother once challenged his mother about breaking up an innocent family, at no point did she claim that she loved him and couldn't let him go. Instead she called dibs on his wallet, saying, "Don't ask me to take food off my table!"

After his visit, my mom simply accepted him into the family, and since then, as far as we were concerned, my father had four children. The four of us hung out together as a family, and eventually the four of us collectively buried our father.

My father moved out when I was about nineteen, and for a long time we didn't know where he was. We discovered he was living with a high-ranking woman at PTSC (long-term relationship number three). He had met her while serving on one of his many boards— this one the board of a credit union. Every year the board would attend an international conference, and for years he took Mummy. Then he started going alone—so he could be with the woman.

Years later, when Daddy was given an early retirement package, Madame-la (as we liked to refer to her) managed to convince him that if he gave her his gratuity to repair her house, she'd leave the house to him when she died. Maybe the sexual hold she had on him overwhelmed his common sense, because he promptly handed over the money.

Apart from being good at extricating money from her lover, she was also into mysticism—or obeah, if you want to call it that. He told the story that she sent him to get a mysterious book on the day she died, telling him that she needed to "release" him before she died.

He was well and properly released, because when he came back with the book, she'd already died, and he found his belongings piled up on the curb. She had never followed through on her promise to transfer the house to him, and her family had kicked him out. Not only was he now homeless, but he was also penniless.

He turned up at my sister's house just as he was, in a pair of Crimplene pants and rubber slippers, toting his Georgie bundle. She told him she had no problem with him staying there, but that he couldn't bring any women into her house. "I guess I won't be staying long, then," he answered. And he didn't.

Next he spent two weeks with his baby mama, but that situation was complicated, as she was still enjoying the company of her policeman boyfriend, so whenever her main squeeze came to visit, my dad would have to jump out the window and run. Inconvenient.

And then one of his adventures turned into a long-standing entanglement with woman number three. He met this young Indian woman at a bar—younger even than my little sister—and she asked him to come back to her home. He was just expecting a little sex but wound up with more than he bargained for.

When they arrived at her place, they discovered there had been a storm and her wooden shack had been partially destroyed. She had four children by different men, and they were essentially homeless. Resourceful Good Samaritan that he was, he gathered her and her string band up and took them to the home of another of his girlfriends, who was out of the country. During her absence he was holding her keys for her, so he installed the little group there for the while.

If in his arrogance he thought this was a nonissue, he was gravely mistaken. A neighbor called the woman, who flew back in and promptly—and justifiably—threw them out.

I can't comprehend why my father still thought they were his problem, but he persevered in his rescue mission, finding them a little hole in the wall in Marabella. And he moved in with them.

It was awful. When we finally located him and went to visit, the home was plagued by flies. This woman produced another child that she alleges is his, but we don't acknowledge him as such because, given Daddy's health problems and her track record, we question Daddy's ability to father a child with her at age sixty-five.

Despite the humiliations my father heaped upon my mother's head, she never lost her temper. She never lowered herself by abandoning the grace she was known for—not even when her rivals for my father's affections got all up in her face. She never conducted herself in any way that was less than admirable; she dressed well and held her head high.

It was no surprise, therefore, that when my mother finally left my father, he didn't even realize she was gone. I guess now we know where I got that skill from. She planned and executed her escape much like I did, saying she was going on vacation while workmen painted and refurbished the house. She packed her suitcases in the car the night before.

When the workmen arrived, she drove off, hopped on a plane, and didn't come back. My father barely noticed, as he was deeply involved with woman number two at the time.

The three of us kids were left behind. Fortunately, I was nineteen and driving, so I was able to do the needful. I dropped my sister at school, then dropped my brother off to work and headed to work myself, and on afternoons, the process was reversed.

My mother didn't have much schooling to start with, because she'd been pulled out of school at a young age because she could sew a dress without a pattern. Sixty plus years later, she is still the consummate dressmaker.

She did, however, enroll in school, and she got her nursing assistant's certificate and worked until her retirement. She actually did very well, and we were, and are still, quite proud of her. She bought several houses and was even able to frequently send money for us to supplement our earnings.

Notwithstanding my father's infidelity, growing up, we had everything we needed; my mother made sure of that. She was ever present and supportive. But oh, she was a strict disciplinarian! I could lime, but I had curfews.

Did I party? Yes, I did! Frequently. Enthusiastically. And strangely enough, my parents were quite permissive with this, never insisting that I be chaperoned. I did what I was supposed to do because that was the kind of young lady I was. And as long as I kept up with the academics, they didn't really fuss about what I did with my weekends. The rule was simple: give them the grades and enjoy my freedom. I broke a lot of curfews once I got my driver's license. And I still got away with it.

Once I received my drivers permit, my mother bustled my siblings into the car every time I left the yard. Was this to keep an eye on me? Maybe. But there was to be no solo driving. The keys were handed over with dire warnings about what would transpire if I played the fool.

Their trust in me was not necessarily well founded, because I do so love to speed. But that's okay; I'm an excellent driver.

I remember that one day, I was chugging along the street with my brother and sister in the backseat when an elderly couple pulled into view. They were well away and proceeding slowly, doing a spot of Sunday afternoon driving (although I can't remember if it was, in fact, a Sunday.) I wasn't worried. It was a nice, flat part of the street.

Maybe they were in two minds about turning, or maybe age had slowed their responses. Regardless, at the very last minute, just as I was right upon them, they decided to dart into a side street—right across my path.

My brother in the front seat and my sister in the back were dead silent; either they were unaware of the danger or they were just too terrified to squeak.

Immediately a series of vivid scenarios flashed through my head—images of the exquisite means of torture my mother would dream up for me if I let anything happen to her precious bundles. My siblings were my responsibility, and the only person who could have protected them was me.

I jammed on the brake, forgetting to clutch the stick-shift car, and turned sharply, winding up alongside the other car, blocking the street. We got off without so much as a ding.

The elderly driver looked confused, and his wife was pale and bewildered. I felt so sorry for them that I couldn't even deliver the Trini tongue-lashing that typically follows near misses like this. I watched as they slunk off, grateful that we had come to no harm, and secretly proud of my skills.

Even a taxi driver who had witnessed the event was impressed. "Good driving!" he told me when he got out to see whether he could help. "They could have killed all of you."

Yeah, I was just that good.

FREEDOM AND
INDEPENDENCE

I remember being asked in high school to select the top three careers I would consider pursuing after graduation. I chose accountant, actuary, and lawyer, and not necessarily in that order. The school then arranged for each student to spend a day with someone in each field, which was a brilliant move on their part.

I was able to eliminate actuary and accountant in short order because they were dead boring. What I really wanted, and what I have wanted most of my life, was to be a lawyer, and then move on to become a judge. That dream has always stayed with me but unfortunately has never manifested. Life happened, calling for some strategic moves.

I ended up with an accounting position, but this was strictly out of necessity. You see, I was planning to leave my first husband, Ross, so I made a calculated decision to target whichever job was advertised the most in the Sunday *Times*. My thinking was that if I were walking away from a marriage with a child in tow, I'd need a career that was in high demand. Unfortunately, that job was always something to do with accounting or business. So I justified my decision by convincing myself that I could go on to do business law.

Before I even graduated, I'd been courted by and accepted into a master's in public administration program at a semiprestigious school downstate. I started off quite nicely when the time came but soon discovered that there was an anchor holding me back. I'd originally filed for and received financial aid, but I had filed taxes jointly with Ross the year before, and because he earned "too much money," I eventually lost my financial and had to drop out during my first semester. I took the punch with good grace, waited a year, and started planning. I worked as a temp to stay afloat, usually starting off doing administrative work. More often than not, my bosses would notice something in me that was different, and I would get bumped up into an executive position. But it was always temporary.

The way I see it, it doesn't matter whether you're an admin or an executive. When you go to work, you dress for work. And I always liked to dress well. I rocked smart, snappy suits that reflected my personality. This rubbed some people the wrong way. "You don't dress like a temp," they commented, looking drab in their vanilla business casual. It sounded like envy to me.

Even my supervisors had a problem with it. "You dress up too much," they'd snipe.

And I'd always keep my cool and quip back, "I would be happy to change my wardrobe, but unfortunately, on this salary, I can't." How's that for a conversation ender?

When I eventually got divorced, I filed again for financial aid. This time, as a single woman. I got it. I decided I had to bump up my skills to make myself more marketable, and in the 1990s, that meant getting an MBA. That was the hot piece of paper in town.

I applied and was accepted to MBA program at another semiprestigious school. One year and a 3.91 GPA later, I graduated and was immediately hired by the university as an adjunct instructor. That was just the beginning.

Professionally Speaking

Almost every sector of any population can claim that they had it hard and that they had obstacles thrown in their way, either by fate or by the society in which they live. As an educated black woman, I think I'm justified in making that claim as well.

I've proven myself, however—and through my own hard work and abilities, not because of knowing the right people. This is why I was so upset with Storm and his involvement with drugs and other illegal activities. I'd worked so hard to establish myself and get in with the decision makers to support my career. Then he decided to act stupid. This is why I cannot—will not—forgive him.

I've earned my credits. I try to stand for something. I'm entitled to respect, and I expect it.

MY FIRST LOVE

I can count on both hands the number of men I have been with. I never slept around, even though I came of age in that golden era before the AIDS epidemic had everyone rethinking their sexual decisions.

There was—and still is—a measure of loyalty that I always brought into my relationships, even when they were going downhill. At my most frustrated, during my darkest days with Ross and Storm, I didn't cheat. I'd rather be celibate than be unfaithful, and with Storm, I was—and for three years at that.

I did date on and off during my separation from Ross, and to me that was okay. But once I went back and had recommitted to the marriage, once we were under the same roof, I was faithful to him until it ended for good.

I've gone without sex for years at a stretch, and it was hard for a woman like myself who enjoys every bit of what life has to offer, including good sex. But I'd rather engage in sexual fasting, as I like to call it, than compromise my principles.

As a teen, my best friend and I dated two best friends. Interestingly, both guys were on the short side. But that didn't matter, because in my teens I was petite. So my beau and I were a perfect fit, or so I thought. But I liked him. He was always serious, his facial expression at odds - with his huge Michael Jackson afro. He was too shy to approach me, which is why his cousins and brother goaded him on. But in that relationship, I was the definitely the aggressor.

Of course, with a boy that age, hormones are in control, and his obsession with hunting and conquering overrode other trivial considerations, such as loyalty to me. With the scent of another woman high in his nostrils, he decided to hit on the sister of a classmate of mine on the side.

His older brother was already dating this young lady's sister, which, I suppose, made it easy. It was one of those convoluted situations—the kind that arise when youngsters hang out in a group and go to the same schools, the same churches, and the same parties. We mixed and mingled, and sometimes changed partners, as the field of potential dates was limited to those we all knew. It was almost incestuous.

Oh, and by the way, this was the guy who took my virginity—correction: the man upon whom I chose to bestow my virginity, because nobody takes from me anything I'm not planning to give them, especially not when it comes to sex.

Losing one's virginity gets so much hype that it is hardly likely that a young girl doesn't fill her own head with fantasies about how it is going to happen, complete with soft music and rose petals. And it's very rare to find a woman whose first experience lived up to that hype.

For me, the big event turned out to be so insignificant that it almost felt as though I was still a virgin after it was over. I walked away thinking, *Did something just happen there?* Even though I had no point of reference that could have indicated to me whether the sex had been good or not, I still felt vaguely unsatisfied. I'd assumed he was experienced, but maybe he'd been a virgin too and, as any teenaged boy would, had been lying about it.

Apparently sex with me wasn't enough for him either. He wanted more, and he had set his sights on this young lady, and they began seeing each other on the sly; and whatever they were doing, they were doing.

And then one day, she had a fender bender with his car, his baby—the car he wouldn't let me drive, by the way. And my best friend, not a stranger from the other side of town, knew all about it but never told me. I can't remember which little birdie eventually whispered that story into my ear, but it wasn't the little birdie I had wanted to hear it from. I was mad, I was hurt, and I was disappointed. I was mad at both him and her, because she was supposed to be my best friend. They had both betrayed me. Interestingly enough, I've since forgiven him but not her.

I retreated into my cave to lick my wounds. He called me after a few days. "I haven't heard from you," he said. "You haven't called. What's going on?"

"Nothing much," I said. We chatted about this and that. I was noncommittal, not letting on what I knew. I wondered how much rope I'd have to give him before he began hanging himself. The conversation eventually meandered around to relationships.

I said, "You have a good heart. If you ever meet someone you like, you have to show them you like them."

He was puzzled. "What are you talking about?"

I inserted the tip of the knife just a little, right between the ribs. "Let's say, for example, you like ... oh I don't know ... let's say your brother's girlfriend's sister. Don't pussyfoot around. Show her you like her!" Then I pushed the blade in to the hilt so smoothly that he didn't even realize it was happening until he was down. "If you ever need advice, I'm your friend and I'll always be your friend, you know. If you have any problems, you can talk to me." Translation: "It is *so* over!"

And that, my dears, is how I handle relationships. There is no cursing. There is no quarrelling. I pretend to lose the battle to win the war. Want to be friends? Sure! Because classy is as classy does.

Eventually my big brother married his girlfriend, and I was one of sixteen bridesmaids. Thirty-two years later, on their thirty-second anniversary, I happened to be in the country and received an invitation to celebrate with the not-so-happy couple. You see, my big brother had always treated me like his little sister, so the invitation was no surprise. I made a grand entrance, having made sure I looked like a million bucks; walked in; scanned the place; and immediately saw my competition, if only thirty-two years later. She, of course was somewhat standoffish with me—you know, since she'd stolen my boyfriend and run his car into a light pole.

I moved through the crowd, smiling and saying my hellos to people I did and didn't know. There were a few older people standing around. I paid them little mind—until it dawned on me that one of those older folks was my first love. *Wow*, I thought. He had not aged well.

He turned, walked over to me, and, true to form, invaded my personal space by getting all up in my face. People looked on with unabashed interest, as if we were part of the hired entertainment.

"How could you leave the country and not tell me?" he asked, confident that no one, not even his significant other, could hear our conversation. I was thinking this was a logical question since he obviously had the deed of ownership to my person locked away in his sock drawer.

"Because we've moved on," I explained. And in my mind, I was thinking, *Duh* ...

"That thing with her," he said, motioning his chin in her direction, "was nothing."

"It wasn't nothing to me." All the time I was wondering, *Why am I explaining this? How clueless can he be?* I was dimly aware that among our spectators was his current girlfriend, and she did not look happy.

Then his big brother decided, "Hey, why not make things worse?" He bounded up to us and said to his brother, "I told her to move on and find someone else because you were playing the fool."

Maybe his brother's influence was calming, because he whined a little more and then settled down. He remarked that I hadn't changed much. He managed to slip in the fact that my butt was still big. He asked me what I did for a living. "I'm not as accomplished as you," he mumbled, seeming to shrink in my presence. "I just work for City Hall."

We took a selfie together while he enviously commented on the fact that I didn't look as old as the rest of them. "Is that right?" I said brightly, and I laughed. Maybe living without malice has its upside.

He ventured that I could stay in touch with him if I wanted to. I mumbled something noncommittal and polite, and then, to his credit, his big brother sent him packing back to his very irritated date. As I watched this insecure old man retreat with his tail well tucked between his legs, I thought, *Bullet number one dodged.*

Interestingly, a few years ago I met both sisters in the supermarket. I noted that my friend was always a sweetheart. I was honored to be one of the bridesmaids. Time had not been good to her, but her sweet spirit stood strong. I also noted that time had definitely been good to my nemesis. At least I used think that's what she represented in my life. In any case, my friend and I hugged, and the three of us talked for quite a while. I remembered thinking, *What a relief Storm was not there with me.* There would have been hell to pay for hanging with my friends. To my pleasant surprise, the conversation was quite candid. I told them how things had gone down between Storm and me, and she jumped in to say that her husband had been beating her, and in that moment, I was able to forgive her. The past disappeared. We were no longer two young girls bickering over some half-ripe little boy who wasn't worth the heartache. We had stared into the eyes of the same devil. We had fought the same battle. We were not enemies, but comrades in arms.

THE MARRYING KIND

When I was in my early twenties, I worked at a bank. And, by the way, if you think some tellers are deliberately slowing things down when you're standing in line, you're a little bit right. Each of us had our favorite customers, and when one walked into the bank, the rest of us would do what we could to speed up or slow down the line so our colleague could get to serve his or her favorite customer.

Maybe it was because he or she always had a kind word for us, or maybe we knew him or her from church. Maybe he or she was just cute and we were in the mood for a little eye candy that day. Whatever the reason, we'd just give the signal to the others, and the game was on.

There was one guy who always caught my eye. He was big, but not fat. There was something about his smile, which made his eyes crinkle, and his manner that left an impression on me, even though our interaction was limited to the few minutes he was before me at the counter.

One day he walked in and the line snaked to the door. It was month-end and a Friday, so the place was packed, but I spotted him across the room as if he had flashing lights hovering over his head. He was wearing a dark purple shirt and a striped tie, looking smart and preppy. Even from where I sat, I could see his shoes were shining. His hair was neat, and everything was in place. I made my move.

I called the clerk at the counter and asked her to collect the gentleman's documents and bring them to me. I dished him up fast and sent his transaction back. "Who did this?" he asked, because getting skipped in the line probably wasn't on the list of things he was expecting that day. She pointed me out to him.

Since it was Friday, we closed at noon to open up again later, at three. I gathered my things, wondering where I felt like eating, but as it turned out, that problem had been solved for me. There was Mr. Purple Shirt, grinning broadly, holding a box of food. *Forget the suit of armor and the white horse*, I thought. *A hot barbecue lunch with all the trimmings is the way to a modern woman's heart!*

We sat in his car right outside the bank and talked as I ate. We hit it off. He wasted no time telling me he had just broken up with his girlfriend. *Message received*, I thought. *Loud and clear.*

We started dating, and it got pretty serious. I remember thinking, *He is good husband material.* He was actually the marrying kind— until the ex-girlfriend started stalking me. She wanted him back and was looking for a way to eliminate the competition. I heard through the grapevine she'd been asking around, trying to dig up dirt on me—dirt I didn't have.

So I turned the tables and started pulling *her* files. I have friends too. I have access to several pullable strings. My investigative work turned up the fact that she was a nurse.

I never saw the point of confronting her, so I had no idea what she looked like. It would have been nice to know, just to get an idea of what I was up against.

In the meantime, he and I were getting on like firecrackers. I had no commitments. I was free to give him *all* my time. We lived in each other's pockets. My mother adored him, and he was a friend of my brother's, although we hadn't known that when we met. He played the saxophone, so he and my musician brother probably saw each other at gigs.

His dad loved me, but his mother hated me. I didn't like this, but I understood. She'd already settled on a daughter-in-law, and here was this young interloper, turning up from out of nowhere, sticking to her precious boy-child like warm chewing gum. She was not impressed and made sure I knew it. His sisters were also split on the like me / hate me vote.

He lived downstairs in his mother's house, so nosy mama was well apprised of our shenanigans and wasted no time carrying stories back to the enemy.

About three months into our relationship, his ex announced that she was pregnant. Strangely enough, the first person he told was my mother. When he shared his news with his parents, his parents told him to be a man and do the right thing. Of course, whether the child was his or not has never been determined; one of his complaints about her was that she loved sex and she apparently got her supply from numerous sources. He swore black is white that he wasn't sleeping with her while he was with me, using the fact that the pregnancy was several months along as supporting evidence. But that promise and a couple of dollars would buy you a bus ticket. As far as he and I were concerned, it was game over.

He was a decent guy, so he married her. I was heartbroken. On the morning of his wedding, he came to our house. I refused to speak to him, but Mummy stepped up and let him say his piece. I could hear him through the door, saying how sorry he was and that he was only doing this because he felt it was the right thing to do. To this day, my mom still likes him because of that.

A couple of years down the road, after I'd had my daughter, I spotted him at an event I'd gone to with my brother. He came over and offered me a lift home. A lot of water had flowed past us since then, so I wasn't as angry. I accepted the lift, and as he drove, we talked. He said again that he was sorry, and he added that his marriage had been very rocky.

"You were the perfect woman for me," he told me. "And you still are. But I did what I had to do." I accepted it and left it at that.

About ten years later, after my first divorce, he wheedled my contact out of my brother and got in touch again. We talked, and I could hear the loneliness and disappointment pouring out of him. They were separated and had been for some time.

He wanted to visit me, and I said okay. It was an interesting visit. We spent the next couple of days together—much of it in bed.

After a long, lazy, sexy weekend, it was time for me to get back to reality. I was renting a beautiful three-story house then, and my master bedroom was lined with mirrors. I liked being able to see myself as I dressed. As he lay naked on the huge bed, watching me in the mirrors, I put on my accessories one by one, making sure that each was precisely chosen and precisely placed.

He watched in silence as I fussed with a favorite brooch, moving it incrementally to the left and right, trying to get it in the perfect spot, and frowning in concentration as I did so.

A lot of our conversation had centered around the idea of my returning home with him. He had become a millionaire by then, and he still is extremely wealthy. He was willing to finance whatever venture I desired. "Anything you want," he urged me. "You just name it. I want us to have a life together."

But looking at me in that brief moment, he realized I was in my element. I was in my own home, surrounded by my things: my art, my books, my clothes, and my precious high-style shoes. It dawned on him that his plan wouldn't work, not in the long term.

"You've changed," he sighed in resignation. "I don't know if you'll be happy back home. It's as if you belong here." In any case, he was still married, and he had been for about fifteen years. That was all a little bit too messy for me.

He left that day, intending to spend a week at his sister's house. I dropped him off, but I hardly had enough time to turn before he called me back. "I'd rather be with you," he told me. "Come back and get me."

We spent another week together, and it was tainted with the knowledge that when it was over, he would go back to where he'd come from and I would stay where I now belonged. It was a little sad, yes, but it added sparkle to the sex and a sprinkle of glitter on our every moment.

About six years after our weeks of romance, he and I reconnected. He had gone back to his wife, but the on-again/off-again marriage was off again.

He'd heard I was here—probably from my brother, who loved the intrigue. He invited me to a gig at which he was playing. I watched him play the sax, and he was as smooth as ever. He introduced me to his friends, and we hung out for the rest of the evening.

A couple of drinks loosened his tongue, and soon he was confessing that no one had ever made him feel like I did and that I had become his personal gold standard for all the women in his life.

Please. I wasn't impressed. He'd come all the way to the United States to find me, changed his mind, and trotted on back to her the moment she beckoned. So what was this rubbish about a gold standard? He accepted my ire with good grace but wouldn't speak to me after.

When I moved back home briefly, I attended a political convention with my brother, with whom this man still hangs. A vanload of red-clad party supporters arrived, and I noticed a greasy-faced woman among them who constantly looked my way but glanced elsewhere the second I caught her eye. It went on for a while; she'd repeatedly look at me and then look at another person in the crowd. I couldn't see the other person's face.

At first I thought it was just another political groupie high on excitement and hype, but the routine went on too long. My spider-sense—no, my woman-sense—started tingling.

"Did you see the love of your life?" my brother whispered into my ear. He seemed to be enjoying a joke I wasn't privy to.

"Who?" I asked, mystified.

And then I heard the laugh. I knew that laugh. I'd heard it while out on the town and while curled up in bed. And if he was right there, then that woman with the oscillating neck, whom I had neither seen nor met before, had to be his wife. In those desperate back-and-forth glances, she had been trying to gauge my reaction to her husband, and his to me.

I wish I could have told her not to worry. All that day, he didn't acknowledge me. I, in turn, had no desire to speak to him. On those rare occasions when we happened to be in the same place at the same time, we treated each other like full buses. I'm not interested in playing any games, and if he won't even acknowledge my brother if he is out with me, or if he won't greet me while his wife is around, that's just rude. You can't talk to me only when it is convenient.

I must admit that I feel a little sorry for her. I hear they now live on separate floors of a huge house. But I don't feel complicit in their problems in any way. She has to accept that there was once something between us and now it's over. *You wanted him. You have him.*

But she's not stupid. She knows he still has feelings for me. He once told my brother that his heart wouldn't let him speak to me, because I had been the love of his life. Oh, grow up. Much later, in a stunning display of male hubris, he tried to add me on Facebook. I deleted the request.

BABY DADDY
MATERIAL ONLY

I met my daughter's father through my sister when she was dating his cousin. My sister wanted to go clubbing, but our parents weren't quite ready to unleash her on the world solo, so they sent me as chaperone. I didn't mind; it was a role I'd played before, and it got me out of the house. So we all wound up hanging out, and there was a lot of attraction between him and me.

He and I dated for twelve years, from the time I was nineteen. About three years in, I found out he had another girlfriend. And no, he didn't *acquire* another girlfriend while he was dating me; he acquired *me* while he was dating his girlfriend. I was the outside woman, and I didn't even know it.

In my defense, I had asked him, on the night we met, whether he was seeing anyone. "Nope," he lied. "I'm not seeing anyone." I accepted that basket full of water without asking any more questions.

Being young and little schooled in the nuances of relationships, I kept on seeing him even after I found out about his main squeeze. I was in *lurve*, and that blinded me. I paid no mind to the girlfriend or the hurt she must have gone through because of his relationship with me.

I stayed with him until I finally realized that this relationship was a dead end. He had no ambition and little education, and neither of those facts bothered him. I, on the other hand, had no doubt that I was going places, and I was already making sure I had the qualifications to get there.

There was just one more thing I wanted from him, and that was a baby. I was just about twenty-six, doing well in my career, and felt it was time. My plan was limited to getting pregnant without getting married, because I had enough sense to recognize that he was not husband material. Apart from his lack of ambition and zero desire to further himself, he was promiscuous. He lived in a town about an hour away from me, and so did his lady love, and because of the distance, I was not able to keep tabs on all his goings-on, but there were many women in his life and bed—a host, a bevy, a flock—and I had no idea.

I do nothing without meticulous planning—certainly nothing as important as having a child. I began laying the foundation. I accumulated six months' vacation from my job. I had built my own house, and I told those close to me that I 6 to know she was planned and wanted and loved from the moment she was conceived.

I didn't bother to ask his permission; I just stopped taking my contraceptive and let nature do what it was designed to do. We'd never used condoms—which, in retrospect, was pretty stupid, given what I knew about STDs and his sexual history. Fortunately, this was way before AIDS came on the scene.

That contraceptive took four years to make its way out of my body. I'd been on it since high school when, in an oddly progressive gesture, Naps took all upper-sixers to Family Planning. My girlfriends and I decided to start on birth control, even though we weren't sexually active at the time. Even more progressively, our parents agreed. We were too young to know about the effects the hormones would have on our bodies, so we blithely chose the one that entailed the least fuss. Six of us, all virgins, began taking our shots.

I had not, by the way, intended to remain a virgin much longer after I graduated. My first love was already in my crosshairs, and the weapon was locked and loaded.

Baby daddy wasn't exactly happy when I told him I was pregnant. I understood why once I found out he already had a bun in oven, so to speak. "You're kidding, right!" was his reaction. But this was the norm, and two babies arriving about the same time was actually a feather in his cap.

In a bizarre twist, years later, when the kids were about twenty, he introduced me to the other woman he got pregnant, and I met her for the first time. She was older, short, plump, plain, and very sweet—too nice a person to put up with him, and naive to a fault. She had no flair, no sense of style, no makeup. What you saw was what you got. That didn't mean she was stupid; she was a successful businesswoman, and boy did she treat my daughter as her own. It was impossible to bear malice—impossible to hate someone so sweet. Besides, I had absolutely no feelings for him, so ... next! It was interesting, though, that when she and I spoke she mentioned to me that, in a bizarre twist, we had actually been seated in the same taxi one day, both of us with our bellies billowing. She recognized me at once, but I didn't know her, so it meant nothing at the time.

In any event, I took the opportunity to apologize to her. "I should have left him," I told her. She was shocked, because we women do so much to hurt each other in our squabbles over men. We jostle and we one-up each other, all as a means to grasping the ultimate prize—the man. But you know what we don't do? We don't apologize. We don't say sorry for the hurt we have caused each other and for the relationships or even families that we have disrupted. I wonder how much better our lives would be as women, both individually and collectively, if we did this more often, or if we even considered the presence of the other woman in the picture before we embarked on a relationship.

In any event, when my daughter was two, I decided to make a run for it and jumped ship.

WHEN MONEY IS WELL SPENT

Over the years, I have consistently outearned the men with whom I have been involved, and I have been my daughter's breadwinner whenever it has mattered. But I stay humble. Financially, I manage. I believe God always finds a way.

I have had my share of difficult moments, and there have been times when I believed there was no foreseeable way I could go on; but over time I've become a firm believer in this constant: whatever the obstacle, God will place the right people or resources in my way to help me overcome it.

For me, money isn't just about survival. It's not about power, either. Money is about security, yes, but it also enables me to add value to someone else's life. It doesn't have to be anything major. Recently I stopped at a gas station and a young man approached me, selling a car cleaning product. He was disheveled but not dirty, looking like the kind of person who could have wound up selling drugs if he had chosen another path. I was so proud of him—proud of the choice he had made.

"Miss, can I show you this product, please?" he asked, very soft-spoken and polite. He launched into his spiel, but I cut him off.

"How much is it?" I asked.

"Miss, let me explain ..." He'd been well trained and would deliver his patter if it killed him.

"I don't need to hear it," I told him. "How much does it cost?"

When he said it was $175, I looked in my purse. I had $179. I bought the product. It was his first sale for the day; he was dumbfounded. It's a moot point whether I will ever use the damn thing, but I said to him, "I'm not investing in this; I'm investing in you." He could have been around the corner selling drugs. As I left, I told him, not unkindly, "Smell the danger. Friends will take you, but they won't bring you back."

He didn't know how to respond, but I hope it left a lasting positive impression. That's what money does: it enables you to bless somebody.

My daughter has the same soft spot for the underdog, as does my mother. When I was teaching at my first college, I had a student who became pregnant with twins. She needed one more class to graduate. My mom had just sold a house, so I asked her to pay the girl's tuition for that one last credit, and she did without asking a question.

RULE 2: CHOOSE THE
WRONG MAN ONCE

I t's actually my mother's fault that Ross and I met. My daughter
was a toddler, and I was going to school while working three or
four jobs, including one at a medical center, one at an airport bureau
de change, and one at a telemarketing scheme where we had to
convince people over the phone to let our employer service their fire
extinguishers. (It was ugly; you don't want to know.) I was beginning
to feel washed out; there wasn't a whole lot of fun in my life.

An invitation to a party in Brooklyn came, and while I was
neither here nor there about attending, my mother insisted. She
was working just as hard, as a certified nurse's aide. She was doing
live-in home care at two different places, morning and night, and
picking up extra duty on Long Island on weekends. So she knew how
hard it was on me as a single mother.

It was her weekend off, and she volunteered to babysit for a few
hours. "You need a break," she told me. "Go out and have some fun!"

Well, the fun started even before I got to the party. There was a
fire on the subway track, and the train got stuck at a station. We all
had to be evacuated, and I stood with my back to a pillar, wondering
when this whole mess would be cleared up and whether I'd even
make it to the party.

The conductor got off and began walking through the crowd. For whatever reason, he zeroed in on me. "Sorry for the inconvenience," he said, with what I came to know as his lady-killing charm. "If you tell me where you're going, maybe I can give you some directions?"

I got sucked into conversation with him, and pretty soon I forgot I was even going to a party. He handed me his number. "Call me," he urged.

I can't even remember whether the party was any good, but I do remember that I called him the next day from my weekend job at a bureau de change at JFK, in what used to be the Pan Am terminal. We talked some more, about everything in general and nothing in particular. It was late by the time I was finished working, and quite dark, so he offered to come pick me up from work and take me home. So far, so good.

The next morning, a Monday, I got up, dressed, and prepared to head out into the world again. There he was, parked across the street, waiting to give me a lift. He'd known what apartment building I was living in, but I had never given him my apartment number. So he simply sat outside and waited so he could surprise me and take me to work.

Did I think that was creepy? Not at all. I thought it was rather sweet. In hindsight, I realize he was probably trying to impress me, but guess what—it worked! I was charmed.

My relationship with Ross was fine, for the most part. It grew on us gradually. He'd pick me up at work, and I'd go to his place. I started leaving clothes there, and the next thing I knew, we were living together.

I've always admired strong men—not physically strong, but strong on the inside. Ross pretended to be strong but never really made the cut. Academically, he was not my equal. He'd flunked out of college, but he never told me this. He had issues with my academic achievement because he was afraid—and rightly so, if I am to be honest with myself—that my constantly increasing education would put me out of his league.

It bothered the hell out of him that I was always correcting his language. He'd say, "I brung you flowers."

I'd say—sweetly of course—"Thanks, but there's no such word as 'brung'."

This drove him nuts. Storm also had the same problem. He'd sneer, "Oh, so you think you're all that?"

I'd shrug and answer, "No, I just like to speak the Queen's English." It's the Naps girl in me.

I was a member of an accounting club, the National Association of Black Accountants, and I went to one of their events in New Jersey. It was mostly men—successful, well-educated men—and standing among them, I could see Ross shrink.

Many of my former classmates came up to talk to me—most of them younger than I, as I was in my late thirties by then. He didn't handle it well. He was peevish with me and churlish with everyone else. I lost some respect for him that night.

Another time, I was working in human resources and there was a formal Christmas office party. I wore a red gown with red four-inch heels with pointy toes ... and no bra. The back of the dress was transparent, with little bridal buttons coming down and a bow at the top. I had the cutest updo, with a band.

My boy wasn't taking that lying down. "Where are you going without a bra?" he sputtered.

I knocked him deftly back into his place. "Excuse me? Do you know how old I am?"

"You can't go out looking like that!"

"Actually, I quite like this look," I said, and I gave him one of my patented "Don't-mess-with-me" looks, daring him to take it any further. He decided not to challenge me, and we went off to the party. But whenever anyone ever tried to talk to me, he'd have an issue.

It was a weakness in him I didn't like. He had no confidence in himself. I guess that, like my father, he didn't think he was attractive enough to get and keep a woman, so he tried to prove it to himself over and over and over. That didn't work for me.

Yet this was a man who loved me. I have no doubt about that. In his immature mind, once I got all my stuff together and I was capable of striking out on my own, I would. So although he began by being very supportive of my every endeavor, he ended up taking every opportunity to clip my wings. *Oh, Ross, you silly bunny. Did you really think you could hold me back?*

Just before we got married, we had a tiff that upset me so badly that I stopped talking to him. He'd park outside my office window, and the girls would come and tell me he was outside. But I didn't give in. He came and said, "I really just need you to talk to me. After we're done, if you want to, you can leave."

He explained that he needed to work through some things and that he was sorry. Then he proposed. We'd been together for two years by that time. He promised to do better.

The wedding was no big thing; we went to City Hall, almost spontaneously, on Valentine's Day. I wore a white hoochie-mama dress, and his best friend was his best man. We were married for ten years.

We lived in his ancestral home in Brooklyn, on the second floor. His younger sister lived upstairs. The place was not fit for human habitation. It was ancient and was exactly how his parents had died and left it. It was dark and musty, and the furniture was ratty. It was like being yanked backwards in time every time I walked through the door.

There was also a safety issue; he would have to come meet me at the train station to walk me home after dark. Even worse, he and his sister didn't get along at all, because her husband beat her, and Ross didn't like that one bit. He objected to the abuse, and she refused to put the man out. She was also sluggish when it came to stumping up the cash to cover the utility bills for the house, so Ross always wound up dipping into his own pocket. There was always a sense of unease, and eventually I had enough.

He told me to find a house—whereever and whatever I wanted. He was earning a lot of money at the time, so that wasn't an issue. I found a beautiful corner house in a nice neighborhood. There was a minister living across from us and a schoolteacher our left. *I could live here*, I thought.

When we went to close on the house, the realtor and I were chatting. I mentioned I was in school. Maybe she was just making conversation, but she smiled and looked interested. "How much longer do you have before you graduate?" she asked me.

Ross butted in, answering for me. "Oh her? She just started. She's got forever!"

The woman gave me a querying look, so I clarified. "Actually, I'm down to my last year."

Ross was surprised, and I tried not to be irritated. Sure, he was busy with running his business, but did this man really not know what was going on in my life? Did he even care?

If there is one thing I can say for him, it's that he was a good provider for my daughter and me. The business was doing well. He even bought a third car, giving me his favorite one to drive—a two-door Lincoln Continental Mark VII, even though it meant that he had to use the smaller one. That's the kind of man he was.

But while he didn't mind supporting my daughter, he could never seem to fully immerse himself in the daddy role. He tried, he really did, but he was awkward and uncomfortable. I guess that, given the kind of demon he was raised by, he didn't have the blueprint for fatherhood ingrained in him. He didn't have a good role model to follow, and so he just fumbled along. Sometimes it was painful to watch, but I appreciated the fact that he tried.

The year we moved into our marital home, Ross was helping my daughter put up Christmas lights in the living room. There was music playing, and she was chattering and laughing. She sounded happy. I was fussing around in the kitchen, smiling to myself at the happy sounds in the next room, the laughter, and the strains of Johnny Mathis. And then there was silence.

I stepped into the room to see what was going on, only to find her struggling to put up lights on her own. Ross was gone. He'd vanished without speaking, like a wisp of mist diffusing into the air. And he was gone for three days.

I tracked him down through his sister, who was living in the place above their parents' old house. "He's downstairs," she told me. "In the basement."

In the basement? I wondered.

"In the dark," she added sympathetically, knowing full well that the subtext of this bizarre news was as disturbing as the information itself. It was year zero of our marriage, just days before Christmas, and my new husband had run aground, seeking out the darkness as if he belonged there. The weirdness of it all sent a chill through me.

She explained that their father had beaten their mother brutally and often. He hadn't taken it easy on the kids, either. Oh, they got their share, and as the only boy, Ross had gotten the worst of it. Their mom had gathered up the courage to escape, taking her four kids with her—and was almost immediately diagnosed with cancer.

Their father told her to come back home. Unable to cope with the disease *and* four children, she moved back home with the kids that summer. On Thanksgiving Day that year, their father had an aneurism and died, and one month later, on Christmas Day, their mother died.

No wonder Ross hated the holidays.

He was generous, though. He used to walk to work and let me use the car. He had a good heart. His problem? Like my father, my grandfather, and so many men before them, his weakness was women. He loved them, craved them, and couldn't get enough of them. And after we were married, he couldn't let them go.

He knew this about himself and recognized his own weakness. He knew at the time that he was too immature for marriage and that he had not yet burned this craving for women out of his soul. But he told me, after the fact, that he wanted me so badly, and he didn't think I'd wait until he had found a way to cast out his own demons.

He decided to put me in the house first and work on his issues after. As you can imagine, that did not work out. It didn't work out for his other fiancée, either.

"What other fiancée?" you may ask. Honey, pull up a chair. It's going to be a long conversation.

As it turned out, Ross the Great Lover had another bride-to-be in Florida, having become engaged before he met me. I was ignorant of her existence, just as she was ignorant of mine.

After we married, this poor girl started calling the house, looking for her man—my man. He managed to convince her, at least for a while, that I was a family member who was just visiting. How and why did a reasonably intelligent woman believe such a lame story, you ask? Because we desperately want to.

"You're the relative Ross was telling me about?" she began.

I must have mumbled something.

She went on. "Well, I'm his fiancée."

Me, "Oh, is that right?" Ten points for self-control.

When Ross came home, I casually mentioned that his fiancée had called. He got that deer-in-the-headlights look. "What did you say to her?"

"Nothing. She did most of the talking."

He weaseled out of it. I let him. My theory is as follows: When confronted with a two-woman-one-man scenario, there are a couple of dynamics at play. Either she knows about you and she's trying to break you up so she can have him to herself, or he lied to her, in which case it's not her fault. I don't jump to conclusions. He swore he'd broken up with her because he was marrying me, so I put it down to dynamic number two: she was deliberately trying to break us up—in which case I wasn't going to waste any mental energy on her.

He did share with me that she was an abused woman with two preadolescent kids, and I guess for her he represented hope. Then one day I found a photo of the two of them looking chummy in a Poconos resort. I couldn't say anything, because I had no idea how old the photo was. Foolish me.

Because Ross worked for the city, during the winter he was

sometimes required to do a lot of overtime. But a lot of the overtime he was putting in wasn't only on the job. Much of that time he also spent bouncing from girlfriend to girlfriend. He often came home late, but that was reasonable to me, because apart from his job he had his small business. He took frequent business trips to Florida, especially in the winter. That gave him ample time to mess around.

Despite his whoring and disrespect, he has admitted that I added value to his life; if not for my intervention, he'd still be living in his parents' old house, which should have been demolished by then. He and his siblings were squabbling over the old wreck, but I told him to let it go.

With me at his side, he said, he'd felt energized and motivated to step up, go into business for himself, and buy us a house. He didn't have enough credit for a mortgage, let alone enough to get a credit card. We used my credit, which was quite good, to leverage the mortgage.

His business took off, and he was soon making US$100,000 a year—and that was in the 1990s. He rented out several rooms in our house, much of the time to students of mine who were looking for accommodation. Meanwhile, he still held on to his job with New York Transit, and I got accepted to college in New York.

I was good for him. I lifted him up.

Speaking of his small business, a good woman supports her man, so I upgraded my license and began driving for him when things were hectic. I once played copilot to him on a trip to Atlantic City to drive a bride, wearing a suit I was obliged to purchase for the job. It was fun. He was fun.

I can't say that job was my calling, though. One day he got caught up at work, and I ended up having to drive a bride into the Bronx. We got lost, and the poor girl was late for her own wedding. She was not happy.

But there was another side of him. He had flown to Florida for a funeral. I didn't know it then, but it was the funeral of fiancée number two's father. Blissfully ignorant of this fact, I went to meet my husband at the airport.

It's funny how I always remember what I was wearing at key points in my life. I had on a long, brightly colored skirt, an off-the-shoulder blouse, and flat shoes. It was all pleasingly bohemian. I watched him striding out, surrounded by a loose group of people, and they were all talking and laughing. I waited for him to notice me. I *knew* he had noticed me. I smiled, waiting for my greeting, my kiss, my hug. And Ross walked straight past me, with just the barest flicker of recognition. Now, I knew I wasn't invisible. My skirt alone was bright enough to use as a semaphore flag. I remember thinking, *Strike two.* The train was out of the station, and there was no turning back.

Nonetheless, I followed, bemused, watching him say his good-byes to his friends. Finally, when they were out of sight, he acknowledged me. It was the weirdest thing. I should have said something, asked a question, but I shook it off. Actually, I didn't; I knew I was already plotting and planning in my head.

It was only long after, when our marriage had failed, that he admitted to me that those friends were relatives of his wife-in-waiting, none of whom had any idea that I existed. He also let it slip that he'd taken her for a weekend in the romantic Poconos—yet another "business trip" that he'd slipped by me.

The parade of women, and the knowledge that I was not the only one, began to wear me down. One day, I was standing on the street corner, waiting on a bus. It was seven in the morning, and there, sailing past me, was my husband with another woman seated next to him. Missy was well ensconced in the plush, warm seat—*my* seat—as though she'd paid for it, chatting away with my husband. I watched them until they rounded the corner and disappeared. I remember thinking, *Strike three.*

Knowing what Ross's constant "overtime" and "business trips" were really about hurt, of course. What he was doing was childish, callous, and selfish. But I also saw it as God's way of saying, "I'm holding a door open for you, girl. Sprint through it while you can."

Did I say anything to him? Telling Ross to stay away from other women was like telling a dog to get off the couch. Sure, he might climb down and slink away, but the second you turn your back, he's up on there again, happy as you please. I didn't waste my breath. I had plans to put in place.

This was one more pillar of smoke in the sky, one more beacon from God telling me He thought it was time I got to stepping.

I try to live my life drama free, and for me, the whole "I'm leaving you" performance was way too much drama for me. I left Ross softly, quietly, and imperceptibly. He never even saw it coming. It was like having termites toiling away in your roof, gnawing at the timber from the inside, leaving the shell ostensibly intact until one day the entire structure comes crashing down and you realize what's been going on all along.

How did I manage? Listen and learn.

THINGS TO DO WHILE
LEAVING YOUR
CHEATING HUSBAND

G od didn't have to tell me twice. I rented a U-Haul and backed it into my mother's yard. Whenever he was off to work, I'd do the termite thing, nibbling away at my long list of things to do while leaving my cheating husband. Slowly, bit by bit, I spirited out my belongings and stashed them in the U-Haul: clothes, shoes, books, mementoes. It helped that we had separate closets.

It took about a month for me to remove what I reasonably could. I knew I'd have to leave the new set of furniture I'd just bought, but I considered that collateral damage. I just took what I absolutely needed for my daughter and myself. Wrapped up in his own selfish world as he was, he never even noticed.

My last exam was on a Saturday. By the Sunday, I was on the road to begin a new life in a new state. My mother kept my daughter and the dog while I tried to find a place for us to settle.

My daughter has called the USA her home since she was two. She was nine when I left Ross. I was determined to make a clean break and move far away from him and the wrinkly old Big Apple, where he lived. I wanted our new home to be the best possible city for a young, single black woman and a child to move to.

I don't make random decisions that can affect the outcome of my life. I don't throw darts at dartboards. When it comes to decisions, I am focused, practical, and well prepared. I created an Excel spreadsheet of all the states and compared them. The standouts for me were Arizona and North and South Carolina. Arizona was too far—and too hot, even for a Trini. I knew I'd get great value for my money in South Carolina, but there was a thriving faction of the Ku Klux Klan there, so ... no.

Cary, North Carolina, had been voted the fourth best place to live in America that year, and that sounded pretty good to me. I got a position in Durham, which was nearby. I upped sticks and headed there.

I shared a U-Haul with another young lady. I hooked my car to the U-Haul and hired a driver, and we drove down in her car. But on our way over, we stopped for gas, got turned around somehow, and got lost. We wound up in Charlotte, North Carolina.

It was the nicest place I had ever gotten lost in. We were surrounded by so much greenery. There were deer at the side of the road! It was so naturally beautiful that I thought, *Wow, I could live here.* I stayed in Durham for a very short time and then moved to Charlotte. It was one of those moments when you know God has a hand in your life and is using even your smallest mistakes to nudge you on the path He has intended for you.

One day three months later, Ross came looking for me in Charlotte, begging me to come back. He told me he wasn't going to give me the divorce I wanted. He even offered to move down and get a job there so he could be close to me. I dug my heels in. It is said that a dog always goes back to its vomit, but I was going to disprove that maxim. I wasn't going back even for milk and honey. If I didn't get the divorce the easy way, I would be getting it the hard way.

He held out on giving me the divorce, like a reluctant mule refusing to pull a wagon. For three months, I asked; and for three months, he refused. In his little fantasy world, I would come around if he was patient enough, if he cajoled me enough, and then we'd be back in each other's arms and hearts again.

But there was nothing, bar nothing, that could convince me to give it another go. I wanted nothing from him; that I made very clear. I wanted no alimony, no property—not a thing. All I wanted was out. And if he wouldn't respond to logic, I figured, maybe he would respond to threats. I found the perfect bargaining chip. "You can give me the divorce willingly or unwillingly," I warned, "but if you force me to take it from you, we're going to have to sell the house and split the proceeds."

That worked. He signed the divorce papers, I signed the quitclaim deed giving up any interest in our marital home, and that was that. I was free again to grow in the direction and at the pace God had intended for me. I didn't realize how cramped and suffocating it was being married to Ross until that yoke was broken. The air in Charlotte never smelled as fresh.

Throughout our ten years of marriage, I never used any contraceptives, because we wanted to have a child together. Yet I never got pregnant. That, coupled with the fact that for a long time he never went on to have any children, leads me to suspect that he may not be able to have any at all. In any case, he never remarried.

I've fallen out of touch with Ross and have no real desire to rekindle contact. I get occasional updates from my sister's husband, who is still friendly with him.

Ross, on the other hand, seems to be more curious about me than I am about him. Whenever he visits my sister and brother-in-law's home, he sees photos of me documenting the progress I've made in my life. These include photos of me in my graduation gowns, earning degree after degree—proof that I am progressing way beyond him. He drops little comments, such as "Her head was always big; she was always a brainiac. I'm not surprised; she always had the potential to achieve." I never got the sense that he was bitter about my achievements, though. He just seemed to accept my growth for what it was.

But he is well off, and that made him a target for amateur gold-diggers out there, so, inevitably, a young lady turned up with a child in tow, claiming that it was his. My brother-in-law swears to me that it isn't, but maybe Ross is in denial. He accepted the child, without even asking for a paternity test, and is raising him as his own.

RULE 3: HAVE SOMEONE OTHER THAN YOURSELF TO LIVE FOR

M otherhood is hard; single motherhood, even more so. Raising a child during and between my two disastrous marriages made life doubly challenging.

I raised my daughter with the same determination and focus I've brought to other aspects of my life. I wanted my child, I made an intentional decision to have her, and from the moment I knew that her tiny heart was beating under my own, I took a vow to ensure she would grow up safe, happy, healthy, and free.

Although we sometimes suffered from the hand-to-mouth hardship that so many single mothers do, I am grateful for the opportunities I've had in my life that have made our survival possible.

I never badmouthed her father, knowing that eventually she would recognize his shortcomings on her own. Smart girl that she is, she did, sooner rather than later; but she loved him anyway, and they had a good relationship. I'm happy for this, because girls need their fathers; they bring something to the table that I, as a woman, never could.

It was difficult overcoming the stoicism that was ingrained within me from an early age—the family ethos that says, "You do not show your feelings; you do not let others goad you to anger; you do not let others see you cry."

The one person with whom I consistently knock those barriers to the ground is my daughter.

Regardless of where I am in the world, we talk fifteen times a day on whatever technology is at hand at the time: Skype, FaceTime, whatever. As she drives home, I can see her drive home, and she can see mine. It's important to have that constant connection, especially since we both live alone and travel so much.

She stays in touch with her brother, too, and I'm happy for that, even though their lives are wildly divergent. He has been involved in violent altercations that his family has never clarified to us. He's been to jail and still clashes with the police now and then, but he has always been respectful to me. I'm vaguely aware that his side of the family tree compares the life paths that the two children have taken, and there is a little envy there, but there's nothing I can do about that. At least the siblings love each other. My daughter even knows her brother's friends. They try to get her to talk to him to see whether she can convince him to turn his life around, but that's been hard.

I don't have to worry about her; she's smart, making good choices for the most part, and is doing well generally. If I have one concern, it would be that she feels she has to measure up to me in terms of all that I've achieved. I tell her that even if she decided to grind to an immediate halt and never pursue another degree in her life, I'd still be proud of her.

She says it was because of me that she decided to go to university in the first place, because she would have been perfectly happy with a high school diploma. Over my dead body! At the very least, I wanted her to get her first degree, which would have put her on a firmer footing in life.

She's an extremely structured young lady, balancing her studies with activities like yoga, African dance, and rock climbing. She takes time for herself and travels a lot, and that's important.

RULE 4: SHOP AROUND

I never thought I'd date outside of my race; I've always thought of myself as being too urban for that. I am too much into Black Power and consciousness. And yet I was once in a relationship with a European doctor. And that experience was enough to put me off them for good.

It was in 1998, and I was between marriages. He was practicing in the United States. His name was Marco—at least that was the anglicized version of his elaborate Czech name, which had way too many consonants for English tongues. I had started my MBA, and he asked one of my classmates to set us up. He wasn't my cup of tea, but he was an interesting character and a great conversationalist. We talked a lot about saving the world. I was more turned on by his brain than anything else, because Marco was—well, let's just say he wasn't about to win any beauty contests. But what a body! Slim and trim. He was an avid cyclist. He had a gorgeous chocolate Labrador called Chocky, and we three used to go wandering in the mountains together, him on his bike, and me on foot with Chocky panting happily by my side. No doubt, he was different.

We dated for about a year. The problem wasn't that he wasn't good to me; he was extremely good to me. When I had a fender-bender and my car was laid up for a while, he lent me one of his cars to drive.

It was evident that a lot of people around us weren't down with the interracial dating thing, and when we went out, we got many dirty looks. He didn't care, and neither did I. We were having a great time.

Then, completely out of nowhere, he came to me with a solemn face. "I want you to keep the car until you get yours sorted," he began.

Still unsuspecting, I said, "Okay. Thanks."

"But I don't think we should see each other again."

There. Just like that, he lobbed it at me, and I had no idea what had triggered it. I was perplexed, and he saw it on my face. He tried to clarify but only wound up muddying the waters some more. "I just don't think I'm good enough for you. You live too clean."

Excuse me? How clean is too clean? And since when was that a deal-breaker? Years later, Storm was to say the same thing to me: "You live too clean." Only then did I understand that this was the protest of a man with secrets—a man whose darkness had filled so much of his soul that he was forced to avert his eyes from my light.

But back then, I hadn't yet learned the hard life lessons that Storm would teach me, so I was perplexed. I pressed for answers, but none came.

Almost immediately, Marco took up a position in Europe with a major American multinational company, earning upward of US$100,000 a year, which made him a millionaire in his native Czech Republic.

Three months later, he called me, chatty and casual, as though he hadn't just cut and run out on me. "What's up?" he asked.

"Getting ready to send my daughter on a vacation," I replied. Then *boom*—the money I needed for her plane ticket arrived as a gift from him, just between friends.

Then another call came, and this time he left me feeling as though the ground I had been standing on had fallen into a sinkhole. "I need your help," he said. And the story poured out.

The nurses were always throwing themselves at him, he began, and I immediately knew this was a story I didn't want to hear. It *stank* of victim blaming. Half the nurses, he insisted, saw the hospital as prime husband-hunting real estate and were ready to give it up to as many men as necessary in order to net their prize.

But either Marco was bored with the nurses who were oh-so-willing, desired a greater challenge, or his ego had grown so inflated that the nurses had shrunk to the status of nonpeople. One night, he and another doctor took a nurse out for drinks, invited her back to Marco's apartment, and drugged her. Then they raped her.

They knocked her out, stripped her down, and availed themselves of her body, taking turns like cats batting a half-dead lizard back and forth between them. She says she remembers passing out with the other doctor on top of her, and when she came to, Marco had taken his place.

The funny thing is that she had been willing, at least as far as the other doctor was concerned. She was sweet on him. But what they could have had by smooth talk they decided to take by force. Being doctors, they had easy access to the drugs and knew just how to administer them. They never gave her the opportunity to say yes or no, or to fight back. She was stone-cold knocked out. By incapacitating her, they gained total and complete control. To me that's even more perverse and dangerous than forcible rape.

And that's why he had been so hasty to snap up that job in Europe. That $100,000 salary was just a bonus; the real reward was having slipped outside of the jurisdiction. Rape charges had been filed against him and his colleague, who hadn't been proactive enough to leave the country to beat the rap. The net was closing in, and he wanted my help.

My erstwhile lover, who had cut and run, leaving me and everything else behind, needed legal advice from me. I knew at once that this was one fool I didn't want for a client. I was horrified, and I refused.

We never spoke after that, but it was a long time before I was able to dispel all the thoughts that swirled through my mind. His change in personality, and in his attitude toward me, had been so sudden and drastic that I can only conclude that he raped this girl while he was still dating me. This wasn't infidelity or an affair with a willing accomplice; this was rape—an assault against another woman *while he and I were together.* Even now, some twenty-three years later, that thought makes me shiver. Did he ever really have feelings for me, or was bagging a black woman just another tick on his sexual bucket list—you know, just below drugging and double-teaming an unconscious woman?

And why did he never rape me? I was always there, often alone with him. I slept in his house. How come he never used force or violence? Is it that I simply wasn't the type of woman he could power trip on? Was it that he needed noncompliance to feel that rush of dominance that rape would give him?

MR. PERFECT—OR SO
HE THOUGHT

A nd then there was Mr. Perfect. When I was in law school,
I experimented with a radio dating system on 97.1 FM, a
jazz station back in Charlotte. It was one of those things where you
phoned in, heard recordings, and got back to the people based on
their messages.

What attracted me to him was the part where he said he was
"brutally honest." That I liked, especially after my experience being
married to the two-faced Ross. So we messaged back and forth, and
then we exchanged phone numbers. He was a personal trainer, so
he looked *good*. He looked perfect.

We "dated" for a year. We were inseparable. I put "dated" in
quotation marks because to this day I'm still not sure what the hell
really went down, because we never slept together.

We did all the other couples stuff: dinners, evenings out, long
conversations. He was fun. We had fun. He even took me to the
Poconos for a weekend, during which we visited that notorious,
cheesy hideaway in Pennsylvania littered with hotels featuring heart-
shaped beds and mirrors on the ceilings. And he never even made
a move on me.

We walked in the woods and held hands. I kept thinking, *This is
the moment. This is when he'll reach out.* But he never even kissed

me. I do remember one night when we were lying in bed together, almost chastely, when I felt something like a finger poking my thigh. I wondered, "That can't really be the size of his penis, can it?" That was as sexual as things ever got, and it left me wondering whether his underendowment had anything to do with his reluctance to sleep with me.

I didn't think he was gay; he'd been married four times and had three sons. I didn't think he was impotent, either; we were both only about forty-one. There was definitely a mental connection; we talked, and we enjoyed many of the same things. But why didn't he seem to desire me? As I pondered, it occurred to me that each of his wives was light-skinned. Three of them were high yellow, and one was white.

Also, as much as we did everything together like a couple, money was an issue for him. He didn't have much because he couldn't hold a job. I suspect that was because he was so inflexible. But he was also kind and attentive. I was in law school at the time, and one day I was in a moot court competition and had to make closing arguments. I'd won the preliminaries, and I came second in the finals. He drove two hours just to see me present. He drove me home, spent the night at my house, and brought me back to campus the next day to collect my car.

Although I was doing well in law school, it soon became obvious that I couldn't afford to continue, so after I completed my first year and bagged a lucrative summer internship, I decided to drop out. But the folks who'd hired me for the internship wanted me around, so they hired me to ghostwrite briefs for court. A year into my relationship with Mr. Perfect, the firm sent me to New York for legal training, to supplement what I was doing. Mr. Perfect took me to the airport.

When I got to my hotel in New York, I called him to let him know I was okay. "By the way," he said to me, as calm as you please, "remember when I told you I went to the club the other night? Well, I met a girl, and I have decided to start dating her."

That coward. "You waited until I got to New York to tell me

this?" I asked, and I hung up the phone. I guess he was afraid that if he'd told me in person I'd have scratched his eyes out. As if he were worth the energy.

I tried to rationalize it by telling myself that we were not, in actuality, a couple, as he had never asked me to be and our sex life together had never extended beyond my own imagination. But that didn't stop it from hurting.

The firm had put me up in a very expensive hotel in Manhattan with all the comforts. It was a great place to be miserable in. I called my sister up, and she came over. I sat in that cushy room and cried. I cried my way through the weekend, and then I shook it off.

When it was time to come home, he called me up to find out what time my flight was arriving so he could come pick me up. I was nearly speechless; this man was as dense as bulletproof glass. It took all my effort, and every ounce of my mother's training, to be polite rather than unleash my inner fishwife. "No, thank you," I told him. What I wanted to say was "Have you lost your damn mind?"

After that, I barely spoke to him. He eventually called to tell me that he'd moved in with Little Miss Nightclub; I'm guessing she was to his taste—a lighter shade of pale. It didn't last. She burned his clothes and threw him out. I was oh, so supportive. "You poor baby!" My reaction was sweet enough to give him diabetes. That's how karma bites you in the ass.

That was around the time that I finished my MBA and met a man called Storm, who would take me through a hurricane of a second marriage. But I digress.

DWAYNE

Between my marriages, I met a huge quarterback called Dwayne. By now you might be guessing that I like my men large, and you'd be right. I like six-footers, three-hundred-pounders—as long as they don't have much of a belly. Big men make me feel protected. Well, at least they did until I met Aamir with his tall, slender, sexy self. Ahh … But again, I digress.

I was supervising at an examination center where students would come from a variety of institutions to take computerized exams. Dwayne came in to do a preliminary exam to begin his master's. We got to talking. I gave him my number, and we'd chat, but I made sure he understood up front that I wasn't interested in a romantic relationship. I have no problem with a consensual adventure here and there, but after what I had gone through with Ross, the last thing on my to-do list was to get involved with another man.

So we came to an agreement: sex, yes; romance, no. That sounds surprisingly cold and clinical to me now, but at the time it was a great way to have my physical needs taken care of without the mess and bother of a boyfriend.

Whenever we could work it out, we got together and got it on. And it was good. He had a huge personality; he was always laughing. He participated in his community; he was a coach for one of the colleges and volunteered at a senior citizen's home. Everyone liked him. I was a few years his senior, but he told me he always dated older women. He was a nice guy, and we had a lot of fun.

Then he went and ruined it by falling in love.

I found out about this when I was doing my MBA and Dwayne's friend and I were in a class together. He reacted as if he were meeting a celebrity because of the way Dwayne spoke about me. "I can't believe I'm meeting you!" he gushed. "That man loves you so much it's not funny!"

I was perturbed, and I filed away that little tidbit for later. Then one day I asked Dwayne, very gently, if there was anything he should be telling me about our relationship.

"I didn't want to say anything, because you said …" He sidestepped and waffled, but I could see where it was heading. I felt bad, for me and for him.

I wondered whether it was that I had been hurt so badly by one or all of my exes that I was so reluctant to get into a serious relationship again. Or was it that watching all the women around me get hurt—including my mother and grandmother, so many relatives, and friends—had caused me to build my walls? Even today I'm cautious.

Many years later, when my marriage to Storm had ended, I chanced upon an email I had somehow missed. It was from Dwayne. I reached out and tracked him down, only to learn that he had died. He'd had a stroke and was moved to his parents' house, where he never recovered.

I felt horrible. I'd been right in his hometown on a two-day conference and could have visited. I still wonder whether he thought I'd seen the email and ignored it, and I wish I could tell him that wasn't so. I wish I'd had had the chance to say good-bye.

RAY

While I was separated from Ross, I started seeing someone. I never intended to get involved with him, but it happened. Admittedly, I did have a few misgivings about being involved with another man while still legally married to Ross, but remembering his other women, an endless parade of them, was enough to harden my heart. He'd put me through too much. "Oh, I didn't start this," I reminded myself. I deserved some happiness.

The way Ray and I met was a tremendous boost to my ego. I was working at the Department of Motor Vehicles, managing the administration of written tests for commercial driver's licenses.

I can even remember what I was wearing that day: a teal pencil skirt, coming to just below the knee; a pair of navy-blue wedge-heeled peep-toe pumps; and a teal-and-navy silk blouse, tucked into the skirt. My hair was permed and styled long.

I was walking through the group of applicants doing the test when a voice said, "Excuse me, miss, could you not walk here, please? You're very distracting."

I began to apologize, but he cut me off. "No, it's not the walking. *You* are very distracting. I just need you to not be within my eyesight right now."

Slick. Real slick.

I had to taxi home on my lunch hour, and as I was standing

waiting on the curb, the same gentleman stopped and gave me a ride. We talked and laughed all the way to my house.

That ride was the thin edge of the wedge. He started bringing me lunch and sending me flowers. It worked. I started falling for him.

He was larger than life, literally. He stood about six foot four and weighed in at 250 pounds. And we looked good together. One day he took me to buy fresh bread, and he was wearing a short-sleeved black T-shirt and black jeans, with a hoop earring in one ear. I was wearing my favorite four-inch black pumps; a short, flared skirt with a white blouse; and a black waistcoat. We crossed the street holding hands, and I remember admiring our reflection in the store window. It was romantic and happy, and I'm sure I was glowing. It was like a scene from a movie.

A car stopped to let us cross, and as they did so, the driver wound down the window and yelled, "Y'all make such an attractive couple!" And his wife agreed, "Yes, you do!"

They weren't wrong in that. It was a good time in my life, and it showed. Even after it was over, every time I drove by that spot it made me smile.

There was a dark side to Ray, though, and I wasn't fooled. I wasn't sure what it was, exactly; it was just a vague sense I had. He'd make statements that would leave me wondering whether he was involved in anything unsavory. But we were good together. We were evenly yoked, academically and otherwise. There was no jealousy, and I never made him feel small in the way I think I made Ross feel small. I know I am a hell of a challenge, but Ray was up to it.

He was coming out of a relationship. He lived with his widowed mother, who liked and welcomed me to the extent that she even babysat my daughter so Ray and I could go out together.

The way Ray treated his mother spoke volumes. He'd hero-worshipped his father; when he was ill, Ray used to carry him around in his arms. He took his father's death badly. He and his mom had a wonderful relationship.

He had no children, but he was great with my daughter. I

remember going to collect her one evening when his mother had babysat for me, and there was Ray, vacuuming the house with my daughter standing on his feet, both of them pushing the vacuum. She was having the time of her life.

That threw me back decades, to a time when my sister and I used to take turns standing on my father's feet as he whirled us around the room, teaching us to dance. That's part of the reason we dance so well.

Compared to Ross, Ray was a natural at fathering, even though he had no kids. And my daughter sensed that in him in the same way cats can sniff out cat lovers. She took to him almost immediately.

One day Ray drove me to her school to pick her up, and as I moved to hop out of the car, he stopped me with one hand. "Don't get out," he said. "I got this."

Before I could say anything, he leaped out and bounded up to the gate, where kids were straggling out one by one. When he came back with her, he put her in the backseat and got in. But she wasn't staying all the way in the back when there was a perfectly good lap going to waste in front! She wriggled through between the seats and clambered onto him, looking through the window on his side as he drove off.

I knew it wasn't safe, but she was gleeful, laughing and pointing at what she was seeing, and he was getting down to her level, acting just as excited by the sights and sounds. It hurt me to have to put an end to it, but sometimes Mommy has to play bad cop for the sake of safety. "It's dangerous," I reminded him gently.

He looked like a kid being told not to play in the rain, but he stopped the car so she could return to the relative security of the backseat.

You know how there are some men out there who should have been fathers and the fact that they never became fathers strikes you as a tragedy? Ray was one of those men.

Ray's mom told me, "You know he loves you, right?" Even his ex got in on the act. She got my number and called me, saying that she wanted to know who this woman Ray was in love with was.

In love? With me? I didn't want to believe it. That was a little much to process. The possibility of being happy, of being in love again, scared the hell out of me. What if this whole thing actually succeeded? I was still technically married and still stinging from a series of infidelities from my wayward husband. I didn't want to overcome these disappointments to put any stock into the possibility of a happy future with Ray. If he was in love with me, what was next?

Next his ex attempted suicide. It was a flamboyant, dramatic, master stroke that got her what she wanted. Ray married his ex. I saw that as a weakness in him; he and I both know he was being manipulated. But hey, I got it.

To this day I'm grateful to Ray because he taught me to love again. I realized that the feelings I had for Ross paled in comparison to those I had felt for Ray. Once I was introduced to real love—real, raw passion—I looked back at what I had with Ross and wondered, "Dang, what was *that?*"

I finally understood that I had been living with a poor counterfeit all along. I wasn't satisfied. The damage was done.

GETTING CAUGHT IN A
STORM: THE HAPPY TIMES

Storm and I met through Storm's niece, who was one of my students. She used to tease me and say, "Wow, you dress so well! Are you dressing up for a man? Do you have one?" And I would shoot back, "Oh, no man can handle me."

After he divorced and moved back into town, Storm met her at a family reunion, and she asked him why he wasn't there with a date. He laughed and said, "No woman can handle me."

That immediately brought me to mind, she said, so she told him, "Aha! I know someone you have to meet!" And that's how it started. She gave us each other's numbers, and he started calling me. I loved talking to him. We'd stay up for hours, talking into the night. He was brilliant, but brilliantly crazy.

I'm not kidding about his name. His parents weren't flower children, and as far as I know they did not pull it out of a Chinese fortune cookie. His father's name was Storm, and his dad, in turn, was named after some guy in their town whose name was also Storm.

The irony that he brought such a storm into my life is not lost on me.

About four months after we met, in December, I had to go to Arizona on business. He dropped me off at the airport, and I resigned myself to not seeing him for a few days. But to my delighted surprise, he appeared in Arizona, and whisked me off to his hotel, where there were peach rose petals scattered on the bed, and all the romantic trimmings. I adore peach roses. I was hooked.

We'd been close but celibate up to that point, and he'd always tried to honor my decision to wait. That was me and my ninety-day rule in action. He'd tried to sweet-talk me out of it only once, and I had stood my ground, so he backed down and let it be. That weekend, though, I capitulated—quite happily, I might add. We wound up celebrating New Year's Eve there together.

The sex was fulfilling. He was a romantic person, or portrayed himself to be, and he had some skills. I think it was the love I had for him that colored my perception, because for a long time I'd thought he was perfect. No, that's not right either. He had his faults, but I thought we were perfect together.

During our courtship, money was always an issue. On one hand, he was almost legalistic with it: if he gave you twenty dollars to buy him an item that cost seventeen, you'd better bring him his change. On the other hand, when it suited him, he made a big show of being generous with it. When we went out together, he always paid the bill. There was one incident, though, that stands out in my mind. We were at Olive Garden, feeding our pasta craving and enjoying a glass of wine, when a black couple at the table next to us started acting up.

They whined and complained to the waiter, sending dishes back, being rude and obnoxious, and generally being customers from hell. They left just ahead of us, and before we stepped outside, Storm popped into the bathroom. I waited for him in the lobby, sitting on a banquette and idly gazing around at the faux-Italian prints on the walls.

The white waiter stomped up to me, obviously in a huff. "Ma'am," he said in a broad New Jersey accent, "your date didn't tip me."

I was puzzled. That wasn't like Storm. He paid our dinner bills, and he always tipped. The cash was still on the table in the room we'd just left.

The man waved the bill under my nose, insisting that he'd been stiffed. "I'm going to need you to add the tip in, ma'am," he said. There was an element of threat in his voice that I didn't like.

All it took was one glance at the bill for me to realize that it wasn't ours. He'd confused us with Mr. and Mrs. Ill-Bred, who were already out the door. I guess at this point I could get into that old aphorism about all black people looking alike, but I'm just going to leave it there.

"That's not ours," I tried to tell him.

He wasn't having any of it. He got more and more agitated, still waving the bill about, hovering over me in an effort to intimidate me. He soon found that I am not easily intimidated. I decided to wait until Storm came out of the bathroom, knowing that together we would clear this up.

He did come out, and the first thing he saw was his girlfriend sitting on a bench with a large, overbearing man in an Olive Garden uniform leaning uncomfortably close, sputtering and waving a piece of paper.

Testosterone kicked in, and before I knew it, two large bulls were bellowing at each other in front of the guests. I'd never seen Storm this angry. He cursed at the top of his voice, drawing the gaze of other diners and staff, some of whom were irritated at having their peaceful meal interrupted by this unpleasantness, while others were thoroughly enjoying a bit of impromptu dinner theatre. As for me, I desperately wished for the power of teleportation.

Eventually the manager came to break it up, and rather than try to determine what exactly was going on, he threw Storm out. "And you're not allowed back in the Olive Garden," he said to our backs as we left. It was humiliating.

I guess you could call it just another red flag, proof that my boyfriend was unstable and unpredictable, but I also saw it as a man standing up for his woman. The fact that we were right—that the bill in question wasn't ours—also made it easier for me to forget it. I almost admired him for holding his ground.

That was one of Storm's special skills—his ability to redeem himself whenever money issues arose.

Storm proposed to me on Valentine's Day, but it wasn't a surprise. We'd been talking about it for some time. We'd gone together to select the rings: an engagement ring, and a wedding ring for each of us.

In an admirable display of gallantry, he suggested that we split the cost of the rings; never mind that my ring was significantly more expensive than his. But I never fuss about money; after all, it's just money. I was willing to sacrifice money for true love. I handed over my credit card without a murmur and without a shadow of doubt.

Even looking back at our trip to the jewelers makes me marvel at how clueless I was about the kind of man he was. The moment we walked into Jared's to choose our rings, the white clerk immediately hustled us over to the cheap side of the store—because black people can't afford the good stuff, you see.

But Storm had done his homework; he was well versed in the four Cs of diamond shopping: color, clarity, carat, and cut. When he explained what he was looking for, the salesman granted us an upgrade, sidling sideways toward the more expensive part of the store.

We narrowed it down to two diamonds, which we intended to set into a ring. They were on par in terms of the Cs but were shaped differently. One was longer and shallower, while the other was shorter and deeper. The first looked bigger at a glance, and that happened to be the one I liked.

Naturally, Storm decided to go for the other one. "No, no," he said, trying out his Jedi mind-control skills. "You like the other one better."

The Force must have been strong in me, because I wasn't swayed. "No," I insisted. "This is the one I like." Fifteen minutes later, he was still trying to browbeat me into choosing the one *he* liked, never mind that it was going on *my* finger.

By then the clerk had turned our little sotto voce argument into a dog-and-pony show, having called over another white girl, and then another. Soon there were three white people being entertained by the sight of two black people bickering over their bling. I appreciated that not one bit. I hate being seen as a representative of my race, especially in such a negative context.

Softly and sweetly, I stood my ground, even when Storm was losing his cool, arguing with me about what *I* was going to wear. "Yes, but ..." he'd sputter.

"Nope," I'd answer, and I'd keep on smiling. He probably didn't know this about me yet, but the softer my voice is, the madder I am. Believe me, heaven and earth could have shifted, but I wasn't budging. After twenty minutes, he threw up his hands in exasperation. I won the right to choose the stone I would wear on my finger, in my ring, for what we both imagined would be the rest of our lives.

Please, stop laughing.

Our next showdown came when we began choosing a setting for the stone. I wanted a halo setting with tiny diamonds going all around, but he argued against it. To him it was a waste of money to have all those tiny diamonds when we could just go for a bigger stone—yes, back to the stone story again.

My position was that the stone we had chosen—well, the one *I* had chosen anyway—already looked bigger than it really was. So what was the problem? But he browbeat me until it was my turn to throw up my hands. I settled for a plain setting. Which is probably why I changed the setting the day after my divorce. I'm not the least bit sentimental about my ring; is an ex-convict sentimental about her handcuffs? I still have it, but it means little to me, so I will probably put it up for sale. It's insured for about US$8,000, so there's that.

Anyway, on that Valentine's Day when my life changed, he came to my house armed with a ring that was already half mine. In the presence of my mother, he got down on his knees and proposed.

Fast forward to three years later. We were moving into the house we were going to share, which belonged to my sister. She'd originally built it with the intention of relocating and then changed her mind. It was on the market, so we decided to rent out my house, as I had no intentions of selling it because I wanted to leave a legacy for my daughter, and he had given me the impression that he owned his ... or maybe I just made that assumption. Again, when we're in love, we see what we want to see. Our hearts paint pretty pictures, and our brains convince us they're real. I found out later that he had been renting his. The man I married had never owned so much as a square foot of dirt in his entire life. Both of his ex-wives had owned their own homes, and he'd just moved in once, or even before, they got married.

There were other red flags I chose to ignore. There was a lady who had mothered me for years. I'd initially worked with her through a temp agency, and since her granddaughter was the same age as my daughter, she would invite us over for Sunday lunch. I picked her up and brought her to the house we were moving into, as it was around the corner from hers, so she could see where I would be and know that I would be all right. "This is where you'll find me," I told her.

Well, Storm must have been going through something at the time, because he was so rude to her! "I don't care who she is!" he railed the moment I began giving her the tour. He ranted and cursed even though she was standing right there. I tried to calm him down. That only made his behavior worse, as if he wanted to prove to me, and to her, that I couldn't control him.

As far as he was concerned, her visit was holding him back from moving in his things, and he had to be out of the house he was living in urgently. Looking back, I guess it probably had to do with nonpayment of rent. True to form, right?

But standing there watching my fiancé shout and curse at my friend, I was mortified. She didn't speak to me afterward and didn't come to the wedding. Years later, after my divorce, I went to her home to reestablish contact. She told me that when she got home that afternoon, she had told her husband that I was too good for him and that he seemed to have some anger management issues. I guess the saying is right: old people can see sitting down what we can't standing up.

But this incident, and Storm's deliberate attempts to alienate my friends and family, was just part of an ongoing process to isolate me. Don't be fooled; this is one of the most powerful tools in the arsenal of the abuser. Separated and held apart from the ones who love you, you are weakened, making you easier for them to control and easier for them to break. It's the same predatory instinct you see in the wild, where the lion seeks out the isolated, the solitary, the frightened, and the impaired. This is when they strike.

There were about 150 people at our wedding, which was Egyptian themed. It was fancy, but I managed to cut the costs. I found a dress online that cost US$3,000, and my mom made it from fabric that cost $10. She snipped bits of fabric from Storm's African agbada—a flowing, wide-sleeved robe—to make my accessories for my neck and wrists and head. His was an elaborate three-piece outfit complete with a hat, and it had an eagle embossed on the back so that when he opened his arms the eagle was in full flight.

Through a series of dramas, we started several hours late, which should have been a warning in and of itself. Nonetheless, the setting, the food, the bride and groom's wedding attire, and the ceremony were all aesthetically perfect.

Our happiest times together took place when we first got married. It was perfect. We complemented each other. It was almost as if he targeted my weaknesses and filled the gaps. Hindsight, they say, is 20/20.

My lack of domestication was probably the biggest gap in those days. While I can't cook for love or money, he was good at it. Even while we were dating, he used to cook for me, and he would pop over and wash my car. Though I can clean if I choose to, I didn't choose to, and so he did most of it.

During our early marriage, he did the laundry, right down to my underwear; he even folded them and put them away. We didn't have a housekeeper, and since he wasn't working (which is a whole other story), he saw it as his way of making a contribution. He was essentially a house-husband.

I was a bit of a workaholic and tended to lose track of time, especially if I was working on a new book or a publication. There were times when I'd be working in my office and he would slip up behind me and put a plate of food down onto my desk. "You've got to take a break," he used to say. "You need to eat." He'd pull up a chair at the desk next to me, and we'd eat together and chat. We were in sync—or at least so I thought.

I was making a lot of money through my consultancies, but it was time-consuming. I enjoyed what I was doing, so it wasn't a burden. He supported me by making sure my technology was working, fixing whichever machine was infested by gremlins, and helping me back up my data. When people asked what he did in his retirement, he'd joke that he was my technical support. He was better than I was at PowerPoint, for example, so I'd send him my edited copy and he'd do the layout. He was great with themes and templates, animated transitions, and things like that. I often gave him half of my fee.

With the money we made, we traveled. I moved around a lot for work, and he came everywhere I went, paid for by the client, as my spouse. We traveled to various cities, and while I was at my conference or workshop, he would go and scope out the lay of the land, so when my work was finished he could tell me what restaurant looked good or what sights we should see together. In hindsight, I realize he traveled and ate for free.

There was one trip he made on his own that sticks in my memory. He went home to his high school homecoming every year without fail. This was the one he used to nag me to go to each year, whether I was busy or not, saying I'd better not refuse. Things had started deteriorating by the time he took the trip this time, and when he arrived, he discovered his bank card wasn't working. He couldn't rent a car.

He called me up to ask whether there was any money on my credit card—which he used because he had no credit. "No," I said.

"What the hell did you do with all that money?" he railed.

"I beg your pardon?"

"Well, do something! I want to rent a car!"

That was the wrong way to speak to me. In the early days, I'd have put some money on the card like a happy little wifey, but since I had discovered he had been skimming money off my credit card, I put my foot down. I have no idea how that little dilemma worked out, but the money certainly didn't come from my direction.

I'd said to Storm more than once, "Let's get Global Entry so we can be precleared for traveling." It's a genius system—a real time-saver in which you are background-checked and cleared so you don't have to wait in those tedious lines at the airport—which can be especially long these days, with all the terror watches and threats. You go to a separate kiosk, where you're quickly checked, fingerprinted, and whisked through. Brilliant.

It made perfect sense to me, but Storm resisted, muttering darkly about Big Brother and conspiracies against black people. I persisted, because as much as I love traveling, I hate being forced to run the gauntlet that is airport security. To me it just makes so much sense to use every opportunity to avoid that. But he stood his ground, and I backed down, silently fuming.

At the time, he just seemed paranoid, but knowing what I know now, I realize it wouldn't have been the smartest thing for someone with assault charges against him, filed by his ex-wives, to submit to a rigorous background check.

But don't let everything he did later fool you; he was a highly intelligent man. We'd have conversations about saving the world that went on for hours. We talked, and our minds met. It was good until it wasn't. His past jumped up and bit us, revealing tendencies I didn't know he had. He was not who he had portrayed himself to be.

In the first few years, we laughed a lot. Once we were driving together, and I don't remember which of us made the joke or what it was about, but we started laughing so hard we had to pull over. Storm was laughing so hard he couldn't drive. I still have that image in my mind.

Those jokes and the times we laughed became fewer and further between—but I didn't pay attention. If I could take responsibility for something I could have done earlier to avert the tragedies that came later, it would be that I didn't notice early enough that things were changing. I should have paid more attention to the fact that he was not as strong as I thought; he was actually a very weak man—emotionally, at least.

He came into the marriage weighed down with the baggage of all his insecurities. Initially my lifestyle was novel to him; it made me interesting. I was an exotic woman who traveled a lot. He got to travel with me and enjoy experiences he hadn't had before. It made him feel like a big shot in front of his friends. He showed me off. But as the marriage progressed, this same exoticism fed his insecurities.

But despite the picture he painted of his life "in paradise," no one ever came to visit—not even his family. Not his sister. Not his daughter. Maybe the gloating was too much for them. I found out later than many of his "friends" didn't really like him, and neither did his close family. They found him a vindictive, self-aggrandizing know-it-all.

It wasn't as though I'd been swept off my feet by a whirlwind, but then again, I wasn't twelve years old, and it had been a long time since I stopped believing in Disney princes. As a matter of fact, if Storm were ever to be cast as a Disney character, he'd be a villain. Of that I am now certain.

RED FLAGS THAT LOOKED ROSE-COLORED TO ME

M ost women who have been in dangerous or horrendous relationships look back at the time when they were happy and search their memories for red flags that should have warned them to get out or to never get in. Often they find many, but they soon realize that the bright red of those flags was obscured by the rose-colored glasses they were wearing at the time.

For me, there were quite a few such red flags—some trivial, some serious. One time, before we were married, I was having lunch with some girlfriends. My phone was in my bag. Unbeknownst to me, I'd accidentally left it on silent. One friend was late, so I pulled out my phone to call her.

There were several missed calls from Storm, but I thought, *Let me call my friend first, before I call him, just to make sure she's okay.* Besides, I had a feeling that talking to him was going to result in a long conversation.

When I called him back—just a few moments later, mind you— he was so obscene on the phone! He said to me, "Between 10:02 and 10:09, I called you six times. There was an outgoing call at 10:07. You used the phone, but you didn't answer my calls!" My girlfriend was horrified—and not necessarily about the manner in which he'd spoken to me as much as about the fact that he could detail my every call to the minute. Red flag! How could I let a man speak to me like this? But I didn't pay it much attention.

It got worse. On a trip to Tennessee, one of my students, a wounded vet, was kind enough to collect me at the airport. He called the house and got Storm, identified himself, and made the mistake of telling him he was going to surprise me by collecting me at the airport.

When I arrived in Tennessee, my phone was dead. The student collected me and took me on a mini-tour of the area before dropping me off. Pretty soon he realized he was sitting on his phone, and when he pulled it out from under his butt, his eyebrows shot up. "Doc, your husband called ..." He squinted at the phone. "Wow. Thirty-two times!"

He handed me the phone, and I called Storm back. Big mistake. He was in the middle of a full-blown nuclear meltdown. "Are you fucking this guy on the side of the road?" he railed. Red flag! Again I chose to ignore it.

To my mortification, my student heard him. He said nothing, made a beeline to the hotel, all but tossed out my baggage, and never spoke to me again.

Then there was Storm and his jobs. There was a huge disparity between his work ethic and mine, to put it politely. He claimed to have retired early, just before the wedding, though he'd actually been laid off. So he never actually held a job during our marriage. And no matter how many opportunities he got, he just refused to work.

When the opportunity came for me to retire to a small island, I took it. At first we stayed in an apartment in a gated community where many professional people were housed. We took our time and found the house we wanted. But my services continued to be sought, so I made a short commute a couple times a week.

A STORM IS BREWING

It was after our move to the gated community that everything changed for the worse. The dark got darker, and what was merely irritating became potentially deadly.

Storm began drinking heavily, and I was naive enough to believe that was his only problem. He'd start as early as eight in the morning, and when I pointed out that it was a little early, he would be defiant. He would pick up drink and ostentatiously look at his watch to show me that he knew it was only seven-thirty, like, "It's not even eight yet, and I'm drinking! What're you gonna do about it?"

If I complained, the next day he'd pick up a bottle at 7:00 a.m. and go through the looking-at-the-watch thing, taunting me. It was juvenile and stupid, but that was the level he'd descended to by then.

By the time I came home from work in the afternoon, there'd be beer bottles strewn all around the house, as if a few fellas had dropped by to hang out, but they'd all been consumed by one man. And his antics became more and more embarrassing.

One evening we were at a local event, setting up shop in a cabana with two other couples, as we always did. I had on a white off-the-shoulder dress, looking as chic as you please, and there was Storm, falling over drunk on the beach before the event had even started. If no one had ever taught me about being stoic, he did. I sat there as if I saw no evil and heard no evil, stirring my drink, pointedly engrossed in the performance on stage. Someone came over and said, "You need to do something about Storm. He's embarrassing you."

"He's embarrassing *himself*," I said with exaggerated nonchalance, "because he's not embarrassing me!" Of course, I refused to come out of the cabana, for fear that anyone would associate me with him! Yes, that was the kind of thing I had to live with.

Even worse than the times when he was falling-on-his-ass drunk were the hallucinations. The first one took place while I was busy with a sizeable project, worth about a million dollars, with two hundred participants. I was extremely busy at the project office.

A friend of Storm's was visiting—a rather strange individual—so he was busy entertaining him. When he returned to my office from dropping him off at the airport, he looked and sounded ill. I put my hand to his forehead to test for fever and immediately jerked it back. Storm was on fire.

I asked one of my assistants to take him home, as I was tied up with work; and by the time I got home, he was seeing Hillary Clinton on the wall. Bombs were falling, and he was screaming that he had to go save the children.

It was the worst night of my life. I had no idea what was going on, and I was terrified for him. The next morning, I got up early, only to discover that he was out cold.

I went out onto the patio and called my mother. And then I completely lost it. I started screaming in anguish and uncertainty. She promptly took a bus, and then a ferry, and came to the rescue, as old southern matriarchs are known to do. I cried for a long time after that, but then the crying died down as Storm became more obnoxious, aggressive, and obscene. It was as if the man I knew was being eroded away like a sand sculpture at high tide.

My feelings died a little every day, and eventually, by the seventh year of our marriage, I'd stopped crying and I'd stopped loving.

I always believe that no matter how bad you feel, you should always dress well. At worst, it will make you feel better about yourself. At best, it will confuse your enemies. As a matter of fact, people who knew me well could have recognized that something was wrong, because I upped the ante. I sported higher heels, and instead of a necklace, I'd wear a scarf. It was a very European look, but I always spiced it up with some tropical colors. If I wore a navy suit, I'd make sure to do a yellow blouse instead of a white one. I wore my skirts above the knee. I even started wearing makeup again, after having stopped because I didn't like what it did to my skin. I usually just wore a bit on the lips and eyes, but now I went full coverage.

Well, apparently this new style sent Storm off the rails. He would shout at me, "You leave here every morning like you're on a fucking runway!"

I'm guessing he thought he was delivering an insult, but I took it as a compliment. Instead, in response, I would hold my chest and, with exaggerated coyness, hit him with a cheery "Awww, you noticed. Thank you!" And I would float out the door as if I were on a cloud of opium. Did he really think he could coerce me into looking like a beat-down old crone? Oh hell no. I like myself too much.

Mr. Househusband even complained that I was spending too much money on myself. I spent money on myself, yes, but I had every right to. That money was mine, and I knew how to make the most of it. Whenever I traveled internationally, there was a boutique I could not resist. I would walk in and, $1,000 later, walk out with an armload of the best styles.

As far as I am concerned, I have earned the right to enjoy the fruits of my labor. I was raised to understand that if I want something, I have to earn the money to get it. If my daughter got up one morning and decided she wanted to holiday in China, I'd take a side gig and make that extra money. I'm smiling as I think back to when my daughter was much, much younger. I worked four jobs then—yes, simultaneously—to make ends meet. I work hard, so I play hard.

If I can't afford something, I wait it out. If I see an advertisement for a pair of shoes I like for $600, I put it in my outbox and keep checking back until the price goes down. But I live off no one. Unfortunately, my ex can't say the same.

Dreams and Prayers

Although I never had any forensic tests done, there's nothing anyone can say to convince me that Storm wasn't drugging me at one point. He'd come on all caring, practically oozing concern. "Sweetheart, you look tired. Why not have a sip of tea?" Tea was a ritual for us, so it didn't seem out of the ordinary.

Sometimes he'd offer me a glass of wine, and after a while I started to beg off because I didn't like how it made me feel. "You know as soon as I have a sip I'm knocked out," I used to plead. I can only imagine how hilarious he found that, but it was true. After two sips, even if it was just seven in the evening, I'd black out, and I'd awaken again at two or three in the morning. I thought that my metabolism was slowing down or the wine was stronger than it looked. He knew I had a sweet tooth, so the sweeter the better.

I dream a lot because I pray a lot. I remember dreaming that I was terrifically thirsty, and as I put the cup of water to my lips, I noticed that the inside of the cup was black. That, I believe, was God talking, warning me about what I drank.

One evening, Storm called me downstairs to watch TV with him. He handed me a very hot cup of tea. It was too hot to drink, so I sat next to him on the sofa, cradling the cup in my hands, watching the show with him. He kept glancing at me. "You're not drinking your tea," he said. There was something in his voice that I couldn't pin down.

"It's hot," I responded. Then he mentioned the tea again. And then once too many. I felt myself shiver.

His phone rang, and he raced into his office, giving me time to replace the tea with water. By the time he came back, I was on the couch as if I had never moved, still cradling the cup and sipping.

When it was empty, I put it in the kitchen, curled back up on the couch, and actually fell asleep.

About forty minutes later, I woke up, and he was gone. I tiptoed upstairs in time to spot him in our room, going through my handbag. Then and there, I had two choices: I could confront him or I could bide my time. I picked the safer route. I calmly sneaked back downstairs, pulled the sheepskin blanket around me, and went back to sleep. Yes, I was living in a Lifetime movie.

For the record, on the day my divorce was final, I had two glasses of the same wine Storm used to ply me with, with no adverse effect.

For the first couple of years, I stuck it out. His increasingly erratic behavior, his aggression, and his reclusiveness all led me to think he was beginning to show signs of early-onset Alzheimer's. I considered it was maybe even some kind of cancer, as he was losing weight.

I was well aware that my marriage was an irrecoverable mess, but I believed in "for better or worse," and if he was ill, a good wife would stand by her man and find ways to help him, even if his failing health meant I wouldn't have a life. I began to mentally prepare for the lifestyle changes I'd be called upon to make when his neurological illness would degenerate to a point where he would require care. I thought of how much I'd hate it if I were sick and he walked out on me. More importantly, I genuinely wanted the marriage to work; after all, it was my second, and I was in my fifties. It never occurred to me then to leave him or to end my marriage. I can't say I have any spiritual or religious misgivings about divorce, but I won't stay in a bad marriage just to save face or to adhere to anyone else's perception of what is or isn't appropriate. But I believed he was ill, and I had compassion.

When I found out he wasn't that kind of sick, after I'd made so many allowances for him and braced myself for the worst, a stone-cold anger rolled over me. It changed me from the inside out, leaving me without an ounce of forgiveness in my heart.

True, it was I who put myself through those changes; he never asked me to help him. But I felt betrayed nonetheless.

His jealousy wasn't confined to my casual male acquaintances; he hated the idea of me spending time with anyone, even when he himself didn't care for my company. One day, on my way back from running errands, I stopped off to lime at the home of a friend of mine, letting him know where I would be.

Twenty minutes later, Storm skated up to the gate of my friend's house, drunk as a pig, with one of his boys in tow, and started buzzing around. A mutual friend who was also there came to my rescue, saying in a joking-but-not-joking tone, "Oh God, man. Give the woman a chance. Do you have to follow her everywhere?"

Another man started ragging him, "Oh God, man. The woman just got here!" And everyone laughed. The message was clear.

His boy wandered off and left Storm with me, so I was tasked with getting his drunk and unruly mess home.

At another event, the husband of an old schoolmate friend, who had a thing for me but who creeped me out, happened to be exiting the bathrooms at the same time I did. Storm spotted us but said nothing.

I was in a bad mood because Storm never wanted to dance; he was always outside smoking. I was so fed up with being the wallflower while all the other couples danced that I decided to dance with the next man who asked me.

Yup, you guessed it. It was Mr. Creepy. I thought, *What the hell*, as it would be my only dance for the evening, so I danced with him. Storm stomped outside and went to sit in the car. A few minutes later, I joked, "Let me go before I have to walk home!" Everyone laughed, but I knew that there was a chance he'd actually leave me behind. After all, he'd done it before.

So yeah, I knew that driving off was within his span of options, but I also knew he wouldn't have gone far. I walked outside, and he was sitting there sulking. I got in, and the thunderstorm he was waiting to unleash on me broke. "I knew all along you were with him! You went into the bathroom to fuck!"

I told him to make up his mind. How many men was I supposed to be with? He hissed and spat all the way home, drank some more outside, and then fell asleep.

It was a long time before it finally dawned on me that alcohol wasn't the only demon with which Storm was wrestling. There were also the drugs and all the unsavory company that went along with them.

I know it's very modern to think that recreational drug use is okay if it's responsibly managed, but I'm dead set against it. Apart from the fact that it is illegal, it can mess you up. We know that. We see the junkies on the street, barely living anything one can reasonably call a life. We know what it does to families. Why would anyone want to self-destruct like that? I don't get it.

Now that I know Storm had been an addict for a long time, I have a better understanding of why sometimes he would crouch in his man cave, go to ground, and wrap himself in solitude. He used to call it "thinking time." Every now and then he would ghost away and stay away. It's a sure bet that during those fugues, he was simply getting high.

Sometimes I think of how my life would have gone if I had had any inkling that Storm used marijuana regularly. I sure as hell would not have married him; that's something I absolutely wouldn't have tolerated. It is counterintuitive to everything I do and everything I am. Even more than infidelity, it would have been a deal-breaker.

In his defense, I don't think he set out to become an addict—but then, who does? I think those losers he kept hanging out with, those characters, deliberately got him hooked so they could bleed him dry. I think he was at first just a weed smoker—a fact he managed to hide from me—and his pushers, or the company he kept, entrapped him by putting heavier stuff into it. Who knows.

By this time, the relationship had unraveled so drastically because the drugs affected his ability to perform this stage play he had scripted for himself, leaving him unable to shrug on the costume of the good husband and play that role.

His weight loss was also so drastic that I had a doctor friend fly in to evaluate him on the sly. She was vacationing in Jamaica with her boyfriend and flew in to visit on her way back home. She stayed a week at our house while I went in to work. While she was there, she agreed to keep a discreet eye on him and report back with her observations. She, too, thought it was Alzheimer's. She said he even asked her the same question three times in five minutes.

I convinced him to go up to the doctor for a full physical, but he refused to take a tox screen—and now I know why. According to my doctor friend, he was healthier than I was: better sugar, better cholesterol—better everything. She was baffled by the weight loss.

And then there was the money. I'm assuming that's what he used to scrounge through my bags for, because finances were becoming more and more of a problem. He began to construct elaborate schemes to get his hands on as much of mine as possible, because drug habits don't pay for themselves.

We used to do a lot of work around the house because I pay the same attention to my home as I do to myself. Storm oversaw much of the work. He managed the supplies and paid the workmen. Of course, that money came out of my pocket, not his. He just informed me how much a job would cost, and I would hand it over without a question.

One day he provoked me into an argument; as usual, it was about my not being around when things needed to be done. He wanted to upgrade the front yard and needed money. "How much?" I asked. He wanted $14,000—no biggie. Again, like a good wife, I completed the bank transaction, handed over the funds, and left for work. I had places to go and people to see.

On another occasion, he demanded $40,000. He reeled off a list of all we needed to see about: front yard, backyard, front door— things like that. The front door, I remember, was about $2,500. "Sure," I said. I went to the bank, withdrew the money, and gave it to him, just a wife trusting her husband to handle something that would benefit us both—no big deal. I documented the door on the receipt and filed it away as I always did.

Two weeks later, would you believe Storm picked another fight and demanded $2,500 for the door? I dropped my guard for a quick second and challenged him. He lost his mind. "Are you calling me a liar?" he bellowed. I quietly backed down, went to the ATM, withdrew the $2,500, and unceremoniously handed it over. For some reason the incident unnerved me even to the point that I began to suspect he was gaslighting me. But on this occasion, as I attached the second receipt to the first, I thought, *At least I know which one of us is crazy.*

That rankled, but I reasoned that my life was worth more than $2,500. I comforted myself with the knowledge that it was almost over—that I just needed to maintain this illusion of normalcy a little while longer.

A few days later, I walked past our gardener in the supermarket. My mind was elsewhere, and I didn't acknowledge him. I'm aware that I sometimes come across as a snob because I tend to be overly cautious with strangers. It's an occupational hazard. I've been watched and followed before and have had my phone bugged. So out in public, I keep to myself.

Storm, on the other hand, has no such reservations; when people came to work for us, it was not unusual to see him drinking beers and laughing with them.

But as I walked past, I remembered my manners and spun on my heel and approached him, asking, in a friendly tone, "Mr. Smithy, sorry. I meant to ask you how much the backyard would cost?"

He shrugged. "Well, the front yard was only seven thousand, so I guess the backyard should only be about ten thousand."

I felt a ringing in my ears. It was as if the oxygen had suddenly been sucked out of the room. Smithy kept on talking, but I barely heard what he said. My head was full of sums and numbers, calculating, calculating. I managed a small smile and a choked

"Thank you," and I went outside to sit in the car. I composed myself, regained control, and went home as if nothing had happened.

Two weeks later, Storm pulled the same stunt. He picked a fight with me and demanded another $35,000. This time I was better armed. Knowledge is a wonderful thing. "No problem, sweetheart. Just let them send the invoices, and I'll leave the checks with you." I stated this as casual as you please, with no attitude. There was no way in hell he was going to call my bluff, so that conversation died right there.

But by then there was no way I could continue to dodge the reality that had been haunting the shadows of every room in the house. I needed to get out. My survival instincts rose to threat level orange; this wasn't just a bad marriage, it was a dangerous predicament. I decided it was more strategic to let him think that everything was okay and that I had no suspicions about where the money was going.

I'm relieved that, as far as I know, he never took anything from the house to pawn or sell. He was satisfied with conning me out of cash. This he added to his own money, which he was using to pay for drugs and alcohol. That spending soon ate its way into our household budget, to the point that he was spending grocery and utility money on things he shouldn't.

I didn't raise a murmur, because by then he had started berating me when I spent any of my money on myself, never mind his penchant for hanging about online, buying himself rubbish like multiple colors of the same new shoes. He'd throw barbs like "When was the last time you bought groceries in this house?" And I'd retort, "I don't have to buy groceries; I pay the mortgage and the car loan. I fill the gas tank when you leave it empty." Match, set, game.

It even came to the point that I got a voicemail from the electric company saying our electricity bill was overdue and we were due for disconnection. I mentioned it to Storm, and even though utilities were his responsibility, he shrugged it off. The man was past giving a damn. "So why don't you go pay it?" he said, and he walked off.

"No problem," I said to his receding back. The next day I went into the payment center and paid off an electric bill of $6,000—several months' worth of unpaid bills. I said not a word. By then I had minus zero feelings for Storm, if such a thing is mathematically possible. I could not possibly have cared less. It was now just a matter of saving my own skin and holding on to my house.

By that time, I'd been celibate for two and a half years, and I didn't even think of having an affair. On and off he would complain about the lack of sex. "You're a cold woman," he railed at me once.

"Well, you have erectile dysfunction," I shot back. Which wasn't necessarily the whole truth, as we weren't trying very hard, but he did have a bit of a problem once, and I didn't mind reminding him of it.

He was drinking more heavily by then, and when he was in his cups he'd accuse me of having an affair; after all, if he wasn't getting any, I was probably giving it to someone else.

Even if I had the desire, he was becoming less and less attractive to me. He went without showering for days and had begun to smell of alcohol and unwashed skin. It was almost like the odor of rotting cucumber, which a doctor later told me was a side effect of being on the drugs. I just thought it was nasty.

It's hard to sleep next to someone who repulses you and even scares you. Storm smelled bad, and it was disgusting.

When I really started to worry for my safety, I put a small wind chime above our bedroom door to act as an early warning signal. After I went to bed, he would be downstairs getting drunk (and very likely high, I learned later). When the chime rang, I would wake up and go on high alert. I didn't leave the bed, but I stayed awake until he crawled in beside me, radiating fumes of alcohol, and crashed. Once he started snoring, I knew it was okay to go to sleep. In the morning, I was up and about before he even rolled over. Looking back at that silly little ruse, I realize that I never truly acknowledged the level of danger I was in.

He didn't push for sex, because of the rape accusation his second wife had made against him. We were arguing about my not wanting to cuddle with him anymore, and I heard him mutter, "I won't force the issue, because the last time I did—" He cut himself short. That made no sense to me at the time, but later, when I was armed with more knowledge, it did.

During our marriage, he was a master manipulator—or at least he thought he was. That's the way I am; I like to sit on my information when it suits me; if I've found out damaging things about you, I may never raise them. I have never revealed my knowledge of a lot of the things I found out about him that led me to divorce him. He still says to all who would listen that he has no idea why I divorced him, as I have never come out and told him, "I know you've been involved in drugs. I know you've been stealing my money." If he's heard anything, he's heard it through the grapevine.

It's interesting how I was able to put on the disguise of normalcy for so long. I love to chat, discuss issues, and minister to other people, and yet in the face of a palpable threat, I was able to keep my silence and refrain from tipping my hand for about a year while I decided on a way out.

This is one area where I hope my experience can help other women in my position protect themselves and even hopefully escape. Once your man knows how much you really know, you've placed yourself in a weakened position. That shame, the sense that they've been found out, can bring the anger to the surface, and you could be looking at physical abuse and even death.

If you've stumbled upon information that could be incriminating for your spouse, the kind that helps you decide that it's time to leave, you have to learn to say nothing. Just quietly and patiently start putting things in place.

Despite all the terrible things I went through, I'm relieved to say that his mistreatment of me got physical only once. I was dressed to attend an awards ceremony held in the honor of one of my students. I remember wearing the dress I wore to my father's funeral. And I looked good.

Naturally, Storm had a problem with this. "Yeah," he slurred, because by then he was stone drunk. "Go ahead and meet your man."

I was running late and did *not* have time for this crap, but I just couldn't let that one slide. "I'm confused," I taunted him. "Last week you said I was gay. Now I have a man? Now you're saying I'm with one of my students?"

In hindsight, it's obvious that he wasn't drunk, as I thought, but high. And this made him dangerous. He spat like a rabid dog and launched himself at me. I never saw him coming, never imagined he would even go that route, so there was no escape. He sank his teeth into my lip, cutting into the flesh both inside and out.

God must have intervened, flooding me with calm and protecting me from further injury. I pushed him back, and he stumbled backward over the back of the sofa. I didn't even look at him to search his face for a clue as to what was going through his mind.

One by one, I stepped out of my high heels, snagging them with one hand as I turned away, and I walked back upstairs to my room. My evening was shot.

I took photos of my bleeding mouth, inside and out, and sent it via WhatsApp to my niece for safekeeping. I emailed copies to the embassy, as we were in a foreign country. I explained that his abuse of me had progressed from mental to physical and asked what my options were.

I made sure to delete the photographs, because by then I had realized that Storm had discovered how to worm his way into my devices and was searching through my files, calls, messages— everything. There was no such thing as privacy in my home—no safe space. Things were coming to a head, and I knew I had to work fast to save my own skin.

When my brother heard about the bite, he announced he getting on a plane to come over and kill Storm, but my mother talked him out of it. They knew by then that they couldn't call me on my phone, so we restricted our conversations to the times I was in my office. I told them I would come up with a plan and execute it myself, so they gave me the space.

Many men go through the cycle of abuse; it's so classic that you can read about it in any textbook. They abuse their woman, whether physically or verbally, and then become penitent. They apologize, offer gifts and flowers, and promise never to do it again—until they do it again.

Not my Storm. In his eyes, he never did anything wrong. I was the cold bitch. I owed him a good life. So why apologize to me? He always blamed the other person. Nothing—*nothing*—was ever his fault.

He may even have thought he was manipulating me all along, because I am very slow to anger. I am slow to respond. So he didn't bear the brunt of my rage until the very end, and by then it was too late.

And then I got a call from an unknown number.

"This is Inspector Bain from the local precinct. I've been asked to call you on a very sensitive matter. We've been staking out a drug dealer in the area, and your red SUV has been observed frequenting those premises. We were directed to investigate further and noted that when your husband dropped you off at the airport, he would head straight for the drug dealer's house. We attempted to secure a search warrant for your house and were told to advise you of the developments."

I cried when I got this news. I was so hurt and disappointed. I'd worked so hard to earn the respect of my peers, and this could have been so embarrassing. I cried for five minutes, and then I hardened my heart and began plotting.

IN THE EYE OF THE STORM

A s repugnant as I came to find him, other women found Storm quite attractive, largely because they were never there when he was dragging around the house in yesterday's underwear, unwashed and smelling to high heaven.

There was one particular friend, who held a senior position at a local organization, who was enthralled by him. "He's such a charmer!" she used to say. She and I would bump into each other at parties and sometimes did things together, such as sip-and-paint parties.

Although many of my friends disliked Storm from the get-go, this particular friend wasn't as discerning. She used to flutter her eyes and giggle whenever he was around. And while our other friends complained about her brashness, she was never quite able to cross my well-laid boundaries—at least until Storm targeted her.

Storm latched on to her like a parasite because he thought she would be useful. When he and a couple of his shady buddies were planning to rent out a house for their goings-on, he quietly arranged for her to visit their little hideaway to see whether she could arrange any financing for their shady endeavor. And no, I was not invited. I took note of that fact but said nothing. I didn't imagine there was anything going on between them, but then again, by that time, I simply didn't much care.

But her overfamiliarity still rankled, purely from the perspective of "Sister, you're embarrassing yourself." At a jazz event a few months later, I was standing around enjoying the music with family, sister, niece, daughter, and half-brother and his wife when she sauntered over. "Hi, hi, hi," she chirped down the line—until she got to Storm, at which point she reached up and intimately stroked his face. Yes, in front my entire family.

I didn't react, but I filed it away as ammunition for when next I needed it, which was soon. As usual, he was calling me a whore, and accusing me of sleeping with the flavor of the month, who happened to be the husband of one of my students. "That's ironic," I reminded him. "There was a time when I would hardly come home and not find the next-door neighbor at our house, fawning all over you, and yet I never accused you of infidelity. You let my friend paw you, and I never said anything. And yet you accuse me of being with this guy? If I can give you the benefit of the doubt, why can't you do the same for me?"

Now, Storm is never one to miss out on an opportunity to play drama queen, so immediately he began doing his best impression of the walking wounded. "How can you say that about me? How could you think I would step out on you? I'm so hurt!" Aww. Poor baby.

It is important to note that Storm refused to work despite all the opportunities that landed in his lap. In hindsight, I realize maybe this was because I was always the one who brought him the opportunities. Maybe it was because he was simply a lazy bastard and a parasite. In any event, he met this young man through my family connections and managed to convince the young man that it was in his best interest to rent out his home to vacationers. The boy agreed and wondered whether Storm wanted the job of managing the house and seeing to its maintenance and upkeep. "No," Storm responded—because God forbid he actually do anything resembling work—"but I have a friend who would be happy to take on the challenge."

That friend, might I add, had been deported for selling drugs. Unfortunately, I learned this only after it all hit the fan.

So Storm's buddy began managing the house, and taking up

residence there as well, since he was virtually homeless. Those little weekend tourist rentals soon degenerated into clandestine parties where sex orgies and drugs were at the top of the menu. Big businessmen and wealthy tourists would drive up through the huge iron gates, which would be locked behind them, and enjoy any type of sex they desired and any kind of drug money could pay for. And Storm was one of the chief instigators.

Over time, the band of miscreants grew as others fell in. They even had a contact with a yacht owner who operated as their drug mule, bringing in the hard stuff on demand. Another illegal immigrant, who was thirty years old to Storm's sixty, was so close to him they called themselves father and son. This young man was hiding out avoiding a rape charge—a fact that bothered Storm not one bit.

THE WAITING

A fter all the thievery, the verbal abuse, and the bite, my only priority was to get out of the marriage alive and with all my possessions. I would be damned if I'd let Storm rob me of everything I'd worked so hard for.

The house would be safe, as I had full ownership, but my private possessions—my clothes, shoes, and favorite items—would be lost if I were to walk out on him with only the shirt on my back. And that was simply not going to happen. So I started plotting.

I enlisted the help of those I loved, those I trusted, and they enthusiastically agreed. I devised an underground railroad for my belongings—a system through which my precious belongings could be spirited away right under his nose, without repercussions.

I started shifting items of clothing and personal belongings I couldn't live without, hanging them in the guest closet. The older clothing that had been hanging there, which I never intended to wear again, I placed in my own closet so there would be no bare shelves or empty hangers if Storm cared to look. I did the same with my precious shoes.

I invited my mom, my daughter, my sister, my nephew, and my niece to visit for Christmas, with the instruction that they were to come with a suitcase hidden inside a suitcase. I asked my brother over, but since he had no idea why I was convening the family like this, he said he didn't want to come, as he didn't want to have to deal with Storm. My sister called him, cursed him out for being clueless, and told him to get it together and do what he was told. So he dutifully came.

Like ants they patiently trucked out my belongings, hidden in their extra suitcases. When Storm commented that my daughter seemed to be traveling heavy, she joked that she was stealing my stuff because my clothes were so cool. "When I see stuff I like, I take it!"

By the time everyone had filed out after Christmas, I had multiple suitcases in various countries and states, waiting to be collected.

I even made a living will and gave a copy to my mother for safekeeping. She hid it in her laptop bag, satisfied that it was safe and secure, until Storm and I went to visit her and he offered to fix her computer—of course, we knew that was a ruse to get into her system to keep tabs on me. He very pleasantly gave the will to my mother, acting as though he had just discovered it. "Are you looking for this?"

But who was he fooling? We knew he had read it. In hindsight it was probably a good thing that he did read it, because he now knew that if he killed me, he wasn't getting the house, and that's probably what saved my life.

Little by little, I set my ducks out in a row. All that remained was for me to pull the trigger.

THE DARK WRITING
ON THE WALL

C all me a sucker for punishment, but I convinced Storm to go
for counselling. Well, "convinced" might be putting it mildly.
What I said was more along the lines of "If you don't make the effort
to get some counselling, this marriage is over."

This worried him mightily, as he could see himself being thrown
off the gravy train, where he'd made himself so comfortable. He
snatched at my suggestion like a man grabbing for a life raft.

He was the one who suggested an out-of-state counselor, because
he didn't want anyone knowing his business. That was okay by me,
because I'm not big on washing my dirty linen in public either—this
book notwithstanding!

I did my homework and found a place that offered individual
counselling, followed by marriage counselling, over the course of a
week. On Monday and Wednesday we had our separate sessions, and
on Friday we had a couple's session. To be honest with you, by then
I knew in my heart that it was time to end this sham, but it made me
feel better knowing that we had gone through the motions, if only
because it allowed my emotional healing to begin.

The whole time we were away, my mother hardly slept. At night,
she would walk and pray, walk and pray, holding me up before the
Lord. My sister was not different. She kept me in prayer, as she

always did. She hated Storm with a passion, and the deeper her hatred, the more she prayed for me. For a couple of days before the counselling began, we stayed with my cousin, and I let her know exactly what was going on so she could keep an eye out for me. She made sure that Storm and I were never left alone; she was always around. She didn't warn her husband, though, partly because she didn't think that it was her story to tell, and partly because he and Storm always got along very well, so she didn't want to put him in a "bros before hos" position. So the poor man wondered why she stuck to me and Storm like white on rice.

She turned out to be very helpful, as I used her house as a transshipment point in my clandestine clothes-smuggling operation. I took three very heavy suitcases with me on that trip, which didn't seem unusual because I was supposed to be there for a week, and given my love affair with my clothes, for me there's no such thing as traveling light. I unloaded a lot of the extra clothes there, and she boxed them up and mailed them to my daughter.

As is par for the course, I paid for both the counselling and the hotel, while Storm sprang for the rental car. The only problem was that as soon as we arrived, he started whining that he had no money and asking whether I could reimburse him for the car!

It so happened that I had just received a sou-sou payout and had US$1,000 cash on me. I handed over $500 without a murmur. "Sure. Here you go." If he knew me as well as he kept boasting he did, he should have found my silence disconcerting. But his arrogance and vindictiveness had gotten the better of him.

He looked at me almost perplexed, as if he expected me to complain or challenge him, and as if he was trying to piss me off. But I wasn't giving him that satisfaction. But you'd better believe he took the money.

I submitted to individual counselling with a good heart, answering the counsellor's questions as honestly as I could. Of course, Storm acted out during our couples session, dropping words for me and throwing himself a pity party. He pounded his chest like

King Kong, saying things like, "It's my house, so she and her family have to abide by my rules!"

"You say your wife spends too much money on her family," my counsellor replied. "Doesn't she meet her monthly commitments?"

At that, he got even more pigheaded. "That's not the point. It's *our* money!"

"But didn't you just say it was *your* house?"

He realized he had overspoken and started backpedaling. "That's not what I meant," he began to stutter, but she cut him off. "Sir, I've been doing this for thirty years. You said exactly what you meant."

He got up and walked out.

I'll never know what went on in Storm's individual session, but it was scary enough for his counsellor to tell my counselor to warn me to get out of the marriage—and get out fast. "Run for your life," she told me, without a shred of exaggeration. As professionals, they'd seen the writing on the wall, and it scared them.

I was glad for the heads-up and was not worried at all that it was a breach of confidentiality on the part of the counsellor. In this business, confidentiality walks out the door as soon as imminent physical danger slithers through the window. "I'm worried for you," she told me. "How can I help?"

"Don't worry," I said. "I'm already putting things in place. The problem is, he has tracking software on all my technology, so I'm afraid to use my phone to call my lawyer."

"Use mine," she said at once, and she handed it over. I called my lawyer and told her to start the divorce proceedings.

My counsellor wasn't the only one who thought I should fear for my life. The police told me to leave and to go to a victim support advocate, but I was afraid that their lack of confidentiality would give Storm wind of what I was planning, and I couldn't take that chance. They warned me that Storm was likely to look at me in a drug-induced haze, see a snake, and come after me with a knife. I should have been way more afraid than I was. That, in retrospect, terrifies me.

While we were out of town, I got a call from my neighbor saying that the house alarm had gone off. There was someone inside the house. My mind started conjuring up all kinds of scenarios about who it could be and what kind of damage the intruder might be doing. I felt frightened and powerless, thinking of all the beautiful things I had collected over the years: artifacts, jewelry, and other unique pieces.

At the same time, Storm's phone rang; it was his boy, calling to tell him that the alarm had gone off. Storm had given permission to this no-account jobless junkie to stay in our home while we were away! And he hadn't even bothered to confer with me first. His story was that he had only let him go onto the back patio so he could use our Wi-Fi.

The police responded to the alarm, and we asked them to switch off the noise. All the while, there was his boy, trying to convince Storm to leave the system disarmed because his car had broken down—a likely story—and he wanted to spend the night in our granny flat on the property, which has a separate entrance. I heard him arguing back, "No, no, I won't do that!" But Storm had already given him the keys. That turned into a falling out between the two men, and that was just fine with me.

FREEDOM

The plan was that after the counselling, I was to fly on to Chicago for several days of professional development, and Storm was to fly home the day after. At least that was the plan as far as Storm understood it. Little did he know that the odds were good that the next time he saw me again, it would be in a court of law.

I flew out of Miami International, buoyed by a wave of relief and release that I would never be able to fully describe, with the bells of freedom pealing in my ears. I know I must have looked a tad crazy, because it was hard to wipe the grin off my face.

You might think that at the end of my marriage, there would have been tears, but by then I was all cried out. The same questions kept rolling around in my head: "Am I really free? Is it really over?"

I checked into my hotel late at night and prepared to begin the course the next day. I showered and dressed up, even though I was staying in and ordering room service, because I wanted to celebrate.

My phone rang, and it was Storm, calling from the house. "You lied to me!"

"What are you talking about?"

"I checked your flight, and you aren't booked to come home. You're going to your daughter's when you leave Chicago! That's why you wouldn't tell me when you were coming back!"

Now that I was free, I could afford to give him attitude. "So how were you able to check my flight?"

"That's not the point!" he blustered. "You *lied!* You're going to see your daughter! When are you coming home?"

I sucked in a deep breath. "I'm not." There it was, out in the open.

He was practically spitting into the phone. "What do you mean you're not?"

Silence.

"Are you leaving me?" he asked.

He was using the wrong tense, and as a career teacher I needed to correct him. "No, Storm. I *have left* you."

Click.

He rang back so many times that the phone started to dance across the bedside table, until eventually I blocked him. He vacillated between pleading and obscenity, but I had little time for either. He emailed. I blocked him. He Skyped. I blocked him. He FaceTimed ... You get the picture.

This continued for a week until I was settled in at my daughter's house. He then called my daughter and told her he was coming up the next day. I didn't want to expose her to that unpleasantness, so I called up a friend on the West Coast, who told me to come on over, which I did. I stayed for a week. I knew I'd need time to heal. I was smart enough to begin using my work laptop, because Storm was already embedded in my personal laptop and able to track everything, especially my finances. I later had that laptop wiped clean. I gave it to my daughter and bought myself a nearly hack-proof Mac. He's still trying, though, the fool.

My girlfriend and her husband spoiled me at their beautiful home near the beach. I did a lot of walking and thinking. I thanked God over and over. My friend was a marriage counsellor, so we had long conversations as she tried to make sure I was mentally and emotionally okay.

But I should have known that fleeing wasn't necessary. Storm didn't have a penny to his name, so what flight could he have gotten on?

Six weeks later, I returned home for the court proceeding. The divorce process had not been easy. He threatened, and then he threatened again. But I held fast. He called my jobs. He maligned my name to my bosses, clients, and friends, telling everyone that I'd had a lifestyle change and I was divorcing him. My priority then—apart from my own survival—was saving my house. I would be damned if I was going to let Storm lay claim to it after all I had gone through, and besides, it was in my name, and I had paid for it.

I'm glad I never blew up at my old friend, or showed her any bad face, even though she would have deserved it just a little. She was the one I turned to when I needed connections to tie up loose ends. I asked her to arrange for my mortgage company to send me a letter saying simply that they needed to see me about my mortgage. That was all I asked. I wanted Storm to think the house was in foreclosure, and therefore that it wasn't worth his energy to try to fight for it. "They're not lying," I told her. "Just say you need me to come in." She used her connections, and for that I am grateful.

The ruse worked. Storm fell for it. He genuinely believed that the house went into foreclosure, even telling a neighbor that I was doing it just to spite him. As if he were worth the effort. To this day, he thinks my brothers own the house.

Ironically, his conscience about his relationship with my friend must have been burning, because when he received the divorce papers, the first thing he did was call her up and tell her it was her fault I was divorcing him, because I had seen her touch his face. Talk about delusion.

She promptly called me, up in arms and boiling over with denial. "But I would never ...!"

I put her out of her misery, amused at the idea that with all that Storm had done to me, this was what he had latched on to as my final tipping point. "Please," I told her, "don't let him get over on you." I even continued to hang out with her after the divorce, because whatever part she had played in that debacle was just a blip on the screen.

I lucked out with the judge who handled the divorce; she was not impressed by anything Storm had to say and was, quite frankly, horrified by what I had gone through. She kept glancing up from my documents and looking at me over her reading glasses; then she'd look at him, asking questions like "Who pays this mortgage? Who pays the bills?"

She was a total bitch—but in my favor. She hardly let him even speak, and she made no secret of her disgust over the way he had treated me and the fact that he had been feeding off me like a leech all these years.

Throughout our marriage, Storm had put on a big show of bravado, showing off and bragging as though everything we owned was really his, including the house. He told a neighbor, "I got the bitch out of my house!" Which was so convincing that when the neighbor spotted me there some time later, he was confused. "Didn't he say you were gone?"

Gone? From my home? Please.

Storm raised the issue of my spending habits in the divorce prehearing, in the presence of both of our lawyers, as if it made a difference. "You're a woman who spends one thousand dollars on herself in one boutique!" he sniped.

"Was it one thousand of *your* dollars?" I asked him, thinking, *How dare you—you, who work nowhere?*

A better man would have heard the warning in my voice or even recognized the idiocy of his words, but Storm is not a better man. He bumbled petulantly on, whining to the judge. "She has money! She can give me some more!" The court was, understandably, unimpressed with that argument.

During the negotiations, he made several truly laughable demands, including spousal support of US$3,000 a month plus his rent, being kept on my health insurance, and ownership of my old sports car. I didn't mind keeping him on my health insurance, because I knew he was sick, and the car had over one hundred thousand miles on it. But I bluntly refused the $3,000 alimony. We agreed to the health insurance, the rent, and the car.

But, textbook addict that he was, he took his eyes off a distant prize to get his hands on an immediate, short-lived reality. He came back with a counterdemand, declining the insurance and the rent and instead asking for a one-off payment of US$30,000 plus the car. I beat him down to $25,000 if he was taking the car, with its high mileage, which I had been keeping around just for its sentimental value. He grabbed it gleefully and ran. I quickly made him sign for it, because I knew I'd gotten away light.

Naturally and unsurprisingly, he wasted no time in taking out a title loan on the car, which is a short-term small loan that brings in quick cash. I can only guess where he spent that money, but with him not having the wherewithal to pay it back, the car was repossessed. And there he was—no money, no car, still addicted: a textbook psychopath who had created his own reality.

He doesn't believe the blame for any of this falls upon his shoulders. As a matter of fact, he sees himself as the victim here and believes the end of the marriage was my fault.

Whatever! My divorce was over in six weeks, done and dusted.

RULE 5: REST, REFLECT, AND HEAL

I think it's important when choosing a mate to find out what you can about where he came from, because that has a huge impact on who he becomes. Who raised him? What kind of family was he raised in? Was his father present, and what kind of man was he? How did he treat their mother? And how did that influence how he feels about women?

If I'd known then what I know now about the way a man's upbringing shapes him, I might have made different choices, or at least viewed the choices that I made differently. Even years after my divorce, it's sometimes hard to scrub away the bad taste in my mouth, especially as more information keeps coming to hand that proves to me that I made not only a bad choice but a dangerous one.

I spoke with Storm's daughter recently. She and her mother were trying to figure out why he hates women, because it's very clear that he does. I learned too late that he beat his first wife for breakfast, lunch, and dinner, yet they are like brother and sister because they have a child together.

He broke the arm of the second, and she's still terrified of him. We didn't move in the same circles, yet from time to time we'd bump into each other. I used to see her fear, and she'd take obvious steps to avoid him. This is a man who, as I discovered later, had had rape charges filed against him by his second wife, my predecessor. He claimed that he didn't see it as rape, but his wife did.

It's an old story—one that hurts us all as women: a victim bring charges, and the accused does whatever is in his power—whether it be guile, charm, coercion, or threats—to have them dropped again. These were all matters of public record, and I would have known about them had I been motivated to check. But when you're in love and about to marry, who thinks of doing that?

This information surfaced only after I'd filed for divorce and my lawyer suggested I hire a private investigator. And that was when, as they say, the story jumped out.

We women are self-blinding. Where our men are concerned, we close our eyes, tamp down our own logical thinking, and silence the doubting voices inside our heads—those voices that whisper to us, "Something's not right"—because we're raised on fairy tales, spoon-fed almost from birth on a watery porridge of platitudes like "Love conquers all" and "Love asks no questions."

Stupid.

Stupid, stupid, stupid.

My friends and loved ones must have a knack for holding their tongues, because it was only after my marriage fell apart that they finally admitted that they never really liked my husband.

It's human nature to feel that we have the right to talk negatively about ourselves or loved ones if we choose, but woe betide anyone else who does the same. "That man of mine is so worthless!" we exclaim, but we then lash out if the person we're talking to responds, "Oh yes, yes he is!"

I'm not like that. When I think of how many people confessed to not liking Storm and to feeling, through a sixth sense, that things were not right, I'm amazed nobody said anything to me before. Friends should be honest, I think. The truth, if delivered with sensitivity and caring, can be a blessing.

I didn't take their comments personally; nor did I feel any need to defend him from their harsh judgment. It was what it was, and as long as they were speaking the truth, I didn't fuss.

The only time I would seek to correct them was when their assumptions or their information were inaccurate. If someone wanted to comment on his toking up, fine. But if I couldn't corroborate an allegation, if I didn't know it for a fact, I'd stop the speaker right there. "I didn't see that," I would say. "I only saw this." You don't get to this age without being impartial, and I see no benefit to me to unnecessarily bashing the man. It's better for my healing to leave it alone.

But I wonder whether my life would have turned out differently had any of these people, any of my friends, taken me aside and said to me, "Girl, think twice. Alarms are going off. Ask yourself if this is what you really want."

I remember what when I was a young girl, still at school, my best friend at the time was like my twin. One morning we caught a taxi to go to school, and I was running late. I forgot to brush my teeth. I sat next to her in the car, chatting away as usual. It was only when I spotted the look of disgust on her face, and realized that she was covering her nose, that I understood the problem. My breath could have knocked over a goat.

I feel that, as my best friend, she could have said something. She never said a word. Maybe she was afraid to hurt my feelings. Maybe she wanted to say something but didn't know how to find the words. Maybe she was just afraid to inhale. For some reason, this made me question our friendship. We were supposed to be tight! Politeness is for use with strangers; the truth is what you tell your friends. Eventually our lives went in different directions. We haven't spoken in about forty years.

Even Storm's two ex-wives might have honored the sisterhood of all women and warned me of his violent tendencies. That would have saved me some grief, but I understand why they didn't. I still believe, though, that we, as women, have to be each other's keepers, even if we don't like the woman who replaced us—even if she stole him from under our noses.

We have to be mature about these things. It takes two to start an affair; the man has a choice to say no. So that petty grudge of wishing the other woman harm is a dangerous waste of time. At the very least, if she is hurt or killed by the man, we would know that we did our duty. We could assuage our conscience with the knowledge that we tried to help. It has never fallen to me to deliver that kind of warning, but if it did, I wouldn't hesitate.

Across the distance of elapsed time, I can see that my entire marriage to Storm was a sham; he was in it for the money and nothing else. In fact, according to the private investigator, he and his niece had even done it before, to his second wife, and he'd transferred all his money to his niece when he married me.

I heard later from the private investigator that his niece was an unsavory character. They'd even taken out disability insurance in my name, using a fake ID with my name and her photo. They were probably planning to convince the insurance company that I was disabled, so they—he—could collect the money.

Storm was looking for a cushy, comfortable ride, and I was it. It was even obvious to more discerning people around us. We once had a neighbor, whom Storm hated, who used to tell Storm to his face that he was nothing more than a gigolo. "Your wife goes to work every day to keep you, and all you do is stay home and rattle around the house. By eleven o'clock you're ridiculously drunk!"

I knew Storm's daughter and her mom fairly well. We've even had Thanksgiving dinners together. She had a baby a few years ago, and the baby daddy was out of the picture, so her parents even moved under her roof for a month to help. That was the kind of image he liked to present—that of being so helpful and supportive.

But she told me later how much she resented his visits because, even though she was in her thirties at the time and worked for more money than he did, he tried to tell her what to do. It was that control that he could never seem to give up.

As for her mother, his first wife, I always sensed an attitude in her when we visited, and it made me feel a little awkward. But after the divorce she finally felt comfortable enough to admit that she had never had an issue with me but that it was Storm that set her teeth on edge. He always wanted to be the boss, even long after they were no longer married, and that got to her. "It was never anything to do with you," she told me.

And that was the kind of man he was—all show, no substance.

I've suggested to her that they should stage an intervention for him, but she doesn't think that would work, largely because he is, in her words, so obnoxious that nobody is willing to work with him.

More disturbingly, she confirmed for me that this version of Storm is the real deal. That's who he always was. The man I married, who used to bring me dinner and make me laugh, was simply fiction—a mirage he created because he sensed that that was the man I wanted him to be.

And I have not seen him since; I don't care to. The average woman might have wanted to shout, curse, attack him, and scratch his face, but me? Out of sight, out of mind.

The taint of Storm's illegal activities still stain my home, to the extent that the police have advised me that it would be dangerous for me to move back in.

How long is it going to take before I can safely take up rightful residence? I have no idea, but I'd rather not come face-to-face with some really bad men who don't care whether we're divorced or not, and who know only that my ex-husband owes them money.

Should I sell the house? Maybe. *Would* I sell it? Hell no. I suffered the last year and a half of my marriage because I was busy putting things in place so I could keep the house—my house, bought and paid for by me. In a few years, when I retire, I plan to move back, sweep out the bad memories along with the cobwebs, and continue to enjoy my life. In the meantime, I rent it out to visitors—the legal kind. I'm happy to say that *my* property manager doesn't double as a pusher or a pimp.

And in the interim, I ponder on the fact that I've gone from a five-thousand-square-foot house with a pool to a room in my mother's basement and have never been happier. This just goes to show you that happiness, like freedom, depends more on where you are in your mind than on your physical situation or your personal circumstances.

During that time, I also prayed a lot. I am convinced that the ghastly experience I went through was never really about Storm; it was about me finding a deeper relationship with God. I'm closer to my family now, too, even the younger generation, my nieces and nephews, whom I can now spend time with as peers. It's good to know that in a crisis they are there for me.

BOUNCING BACK

People who haven't seen me since the divorce tell me I look younger, and I do. I feel younger. I act younger. I hang out with nieces and nephews in their twenties and thirties at parties and feel no different from them.

A great burden has been lifted, and I've become a new person. My mother says I smile too much. Maybe I do! And it doesn't go unnoticed by others who are happy to comment on the difference.

When anyone engages me in a serious conversation and dares to ask me, "How did you handle it? How did you put up with that and stay so positive?" I answer, "Because I knew it was his problem and not mine. I wasn't the one on drugs, so I refused to let his problem dictate how I lived my life."

The infrequent response is "That's an interesting approach. But how do you bounce back?"

"Girl, please," I say cheerily. "I've already found myself a little cutie pie!" And we all crack up. "I'm the consummate romantic," I go on, "and I will always be. Life goes on. You need to shake yourself up. Unless you want to be miserable for the rest of your life, let it the hell go, or he will always control you."

It's good when women share their experiences; when we do so, we lighten each other's burdens. We're educated women; why do we take this crap? Some of my high school sista girls even think that we have a higher divorce rate than women from other prestigious schools. Why? Because we were raised to stand up for ourselves, and we do.

THE SISTERHOOD

There's something special about friendships between women that allows them to last. One of the most important foundations for me is loyalty. Good friendships are also based on trust and honesty. A good friendship is a judgment-free zone. That said, though, I never shared with them anything that was going on between me and Storm until well after the fact. I chalk that up to my innate reserve and my desire for privacy overcoming the need to share.

But the more I speak to women now, after what I've gone through, the more I realize how important it is for us to rise above any of the stupid little barriers we let stand between us, and to talk our way through this terrible morass of dark secrets that is plaguing women of all ages. And one powerful way to do this is for us to be each other's friends, advisors, and even saviors if necessary. You can't get around the fact that when women are friends, things happen.

The year after my divorce, I happened to bump into my dressmaker, a very talented woman I hadn't seen in a long time, even though she was still holding several items for me. We fell out of touch when I was divorcing Storm; I was so busy trying to get away from him that I lost contact with several friends.

She'd met my husband, and she asked me about him. "Actually, we got divorced," I told her.

She was surprised. "Oh, my God, really? He seemed like such a nice gentleman!"

Ha, I thought. "Come see me" and "come live with me" are two different things. "Yes, everybody would quite agree that he seemed to be a nice person," I hedged.

"He stepped out on you, or what?" she asked, because of course, in everyone's minds, infidelity is the default setting for grounds for divorce. "No," I said, "he actually didn't. I wish it was as simple as that!" I told her what happened. We started talking about the different manifestations of abuse and the fact that a lot of people make the mistake of thinking that abuse is only physical. In my mind, sometimes psychological and emotional abuse are worse.

Immediately, as has happened so many times with women I've met since, she spilled the beans on her own marriage. Her life with her husband was so violent, she told me, that at one time she slept with a hammer under her pillow for her own protection. This is a smart woman—a stylish, talented woman with so much going for her. And she feared for her life.

Tragically, her sister is going through the same thing, to the extent that her sister's son committed suicide because he couldn't bear to look on anymore at the horror his mother was enduring.

Another classmate of mine shared that she had major surgery and her husband dutifully brought her home and tucked her into bed. Then he dressed to leave. "Where are you going?" she asked, bewildered. "I'm not your fucking nursemaid" was his response. And he swanned off, leaving her alone.

Some time later, she found the receipt for the hotel where he had spent the night with his "companion," for want of a more discreet word. I ask, again, and again, why do so many of us, bright, bold, beautiful women end up with men like these?

I've said openly, several times, that I wouldn't stay in a bad marriage and that I didn't understand why any woman would. Well, who told me to say that out loud? I've lost a few friends as a result.

I'm realizing more and more that many women do stay in bad marriages, whether it's because of children, because they would be ashamed to admit that their marriage had failed, or for so many other reasons.

My girlfriend who had been abandoned by her husband after coming home from surgery attempted to file for divorce, only to discover that the process was, in fact, cost prohibitive and that they would have to sell the house and split the proceeds. Her courage failed her. She was about to retire, and money would be tight. She decided to remain in the house and share it with him. She has one floor, and he has another. She does her own thing, and he does his. That's my idea of purgatory.

And if that is not bad enough, sometimes the way women compete against each other drives me crazy. I have female acquaintances who constantly monitor me, my travels, and my relationships and ask question after question. But the questions aren't meant to determine whether I'm okay or whether there's an area in my life they can support me in. It's purely a way to measure where they are against where I am in life. We constantly compare what each woman has against what we have. That sense of competition between women drives me nuts. Why do we do that to each other?

WHEN YOU ARE
UNEQUALLY YOKED

One of the most important concepts a modern woman has to learn is that of being equally yoked. The Bible speaks about it in terms of faith, warning Christians not to marry unbelievers. The phrase evokes the image of a strong ox and a weak one yoked together and attempting to plough a field. It does not work. While one animal surges ahead, the other stumbles and is dragged. Soon the stronger one, too, falls to its knees.

But I want to say something to all women: this inequality doesn't stop at religion; it extends to education, upbringing, occupation, and pedigree. Yoking yourself to the wrong man, through relationships, sex, marriage, or child-rearing, can cause you to stumble and even fall.

Sometimes, when it comes to men, I think I'm too picky. My daughter constantly accused me of judging by pedigree. "Yes, I do," I agreed. "But let's be realistic. A truck driver may look good on the surface, but if he has no conversation to offer, what do you think is going to happen? There has to be a meeting of the minds. It doesn't have to be an academic match; you can have a truck driver who's brilliant, but your minds must meet."

Maybe it's a reaction to the experiences I have had in the past, or maybe it's simply because that is the kind of woman I am. I have high expectations of myself and work hard to fulfil those expectations, so I am not disappointed. So why is it unreasonable to expect a man to place similar demands on himself? Because if he doesn't go all-out to live up to his own expectations, how can I expect him to live up to mine?

Up until this point, I have not allowed pedigree to drive my choices; but believe me, going forward, I will not be making that mistake again. My daughter's father wasn't particularly educated. My first husband was a subway conductor, and Storm at least had a college degree. But fat good that did. Now, because of my experience with Storm, where I once challenged the idea of "marrying down" or getting into relationships with men who were somehow beneath my station, I plan to wholeheartedly apply the pedigree test going forward.

I try not to judge others, but what interests me is your pedigree, not your station. For me that's more important and is a greater indication of character. Who raised you? What did they teach you? Where are you going? How do you live your life?

My daughter laughs at me for that, but I want her to benefit from the wisdom of the mistakes I've made without having to make them herself. "You need to be equally yoked," I always tell her. She's not buying it, and I guess at age thirty maybe I wouldn't have myself.

We all have to start somewhere. I was nineteen when I met her father, and he was *fine*. What he did didn't matter, and at the time I was just starting out in the working world myself. When I met my first husband, I had just begun my undergrad studies.

With Storm, though, I most certainly married down, but that manifested only after the marriage was well under way. He worked in corporate America when I met him, and he absolutely portrayed himself as more than he was.

I'd just finished my MBA, and we dated throughout my PhD studies. As a matter of fact, I missed my own graduation, as I was on my honeymoon. Then Storm got laid off—although the story he put out at the time was that he took early retirement. The financial fallout of that incident only underscored the disparity between us.

The problem of being unevenly yoked presents itself when we, as professional women, grow and our men do not. It's important for us to be lifelong learners, because when you educate yourself, your thinking changes. If your thinking changes and your man's doesn't, there's a problem.

Many, many years later, my daughter's father is the exact same person he was when I met him at nineteen. It's like a time warp. He still talks like a boy and wears ridiculous clothes and lashings of gold jewelry. My sister's husband is the same person he was thirty years ago when they first met, and my sister most assuredly is not.

We women need to bear this in mind when we choose. And please, don't marry someone because of his potential, which is something we tend to do, because what happens if that potential never manifests? You become resentful, and he becomes resentful of your potential manifesting when his hasn't.

On the surface, Storm pretended to be so proud of my achievements. He'd boast of me to his friends, but when the truth of his addiction came out, I learned how much he hated me for putting him in the shade. He said, "You think because you have several fucking degrees you're all that, but you ain't fucking shit." And there it was, bare and naked, for everyone to see.

PLENTY OF FISH

My daughter and her best friend must have decided that I was way too much woman to go to waste, because they signed me up on an online dating site. How cute.

For two months I browsed the paltry offerings, saying "yuck" at almost everything I saw. Then, the night before I flew out of the country, a man messaged me. "I love your pictures. I love your profile."

I'd deliberately posted photos of myself doing unusual things all over the world: me scuba diving in the Caribbean, me in a hot air balloon in Australia. I was showing my adventurous side, making a declaration that I am not ordinary and will never see myself as ordinary. It was my attempt at eliminating what I call "truck drivers" (no disrespect meant).

"I'd like us to meet," he said, still unaware of the connection. "Here's my number; would you call me?"

Hell yeah, I called him. We talked for hours. I told him I was going to be at an event he was going to, and I gave him my number. By the time I was on the ground the next day, he had already called me and left a message.

We talked again on the phone that night; he even wanted me to come out to meet him in person, but I was jet-lagged and it was late. Besides, I could feel an excitement growing in me—a sense inside myself that something big was happening here, so I bided my time. I chose to delay my gratification and build my excitement.

He asked me to lunch the next day. The chemistry was instantaneous; the attraction hit us both like a bolt. The moment he got to his feet to greet me, I looked him over from his feet and up, up, up, thinking that this height would never end. He was so fine!

After lunch we decided to spend the afternoon together. He rode with me to a small lake outside of the city, where we sat, chatted, and watched the wild birds flit past. We had the rest of the day stretching before us and wanted to relish every moment of it.

As he got into the car, he gave me a gentle kiss on my cheek and then turned my head to give me an even gentler kiss on my lips. "I've been wanting to do that all afternoon," he said with a mischievous grin, "but I didn't want to overstep."

Oh, you should have overstepped, brother! I thought, *if that was what you had waiting for me!*

He then settled back into his seat without another word, placed his hand behind my head, and gently massaged the back of my head until we stopped at a traffic signal. Then he bent over and gave me a deep, deep, thought-provoking, bone chilling kiss—and he did that at every stop thereafter.

In total, we spent seven hours together. Three hours into the date, my daughter called, more curious than concerned. "It's not like you to not check in. Who are you with?" I laughed. That's my girl. She knows me so well. I hadn't told her I was going to meet my online prospect.

I guess that might sound unsafe, but I'm not stupid; lunch and the lake were both in public, well-populated spaces, and I never felt as though I was at risk. My phone was on speaker, and Aamir must have sensed the thread of worry in her voice, because he introduced himself, even offering, in complete seriousness, his driver's license number.

This put my daughter immediately at ease. "Well, if you have occupied my mother's time for all these hours, I need you to come to the house tomorrow. I have forty questions to ask you."

"Yes ma'am," he said.

Full marks, I thought. *Full marks.*

It was time to part, as he had to leave to take his mother to the ball.

Everything else was a blur. We chatted about everything under the sun, our conversation interspersed with stop-light kisses. Later he sent me a picture of him and his mom having a great time, and when he got back, he called, even though the witching hour was upon us. We talked into the early hours of the morning. It was incredible; we couldn't get enough of each other, and neither of us was ready to fall asleep and lose a minute of conversation.

The next day, at the graduation ceremony, I filed in with the other parents and took my place. *Ding!* A text came through.

Good morning sweetheart! Where are you seated?

I'm in section 124.

I'm in 129.

Meet me in the hallway.

I stepped out into the hall, where he was already waiting. I walked up to him, happy to see him even though it had been only a few hours since we parted, and fewer still since our overnight gabfest on the phone.

And he bent down and gave me another deep, thought-provoking kiss, in front of thousands of people milling around. My immediate thought was *I guess you have nothing to hide.*

I went back to my seat, and he went back to his. I texted him my daughter's address, where the family would be celebrating afterward. He texted back, "Does she need me to bring anything?"

Was he well-bred or what?

"No, she's fine," I responded. And then I squirmed in anticipation all through the graduation ceremony. This was something different; I could feel it deep inside. This was going to be special.

I was in the kitchen when he arrived; my daughter greeted him at the door. They talked for a while, and then she wrangled him inside, introducing him to everyone—taking control, as she always does.

When he finally made it inside, I turned around to face him and, you guessed it, he planted a kiss on me in front of all witnesses. It must have made as great an impression on everyone else as it did on me, because my daughter's pastor sitting nearby couldn't help but tease me. "Where did you get that cutie pie?"

I hoped nobody could see the heat in my face, and I laughed. "You don't want to know."

I served his lunch—no wisecracks about taking out a man's food, please—and he poured two glasses and followed me upstairs. Mummy was up there, and the two of them talked for about an hour, as natural as you please. They're both diabetic, so they swapped war stories and shared advice on home remedies, and there I was, the third wheel, but not minding it one bit.

She eventually retired to her room, leaving us youngsters to our own devices. We talked and kissed, and talked and kissed, until he had lipstick all over his face. Mom popped out to use the bathroom and busted him dead to rights. "You might want to wipe your face before you go downstairs," she warned him. He flushed but obediently scrubbed away the tell-tale marks.

Later she would tell me that she really liked him. The only other man in my life that she had liked that much, she said, was real husband material, because he had had the courtesy to talk to her about the situation he'd gotten himself into with Ruth.

My daughter liked him too, and that's important to me, not only because I want her to appreciate someone I care about but also because she's a bright and perceptive young lady, and I value her opinion.

The party started to wind down, and Aamir prepared to leave. It had been a great day; I was glad to see him, and gladder still that so many people I respect and care about seemed to like him. I almost wished it didn't have to come to an end. He was flying back home the next morning. I missed him already.

As we said our good-byes, I felt him touch my hand. "No pressure," he said, just softly enough that only I could hear. I was puzzled, but when I looked in my hand, I understood. It was the key card to his hotel room.

And there I was, with a key in my hand and a decision to make. I'd been celibate for four years by then, and to be honest, I could have continued in the same vein if I chose. I'm like that; as sexual as I am, as much as I enjoy it, I can shut off the valve if necessary.

But I can also open the floodgates if necessary. It didn't take long to make a decision. I shared it with my mom, because she has always been my sounding board, and we didn't have any secrets.

"You know what?" I told her. "It's been too long. I'm going, and I'm gonna give it up."

Mummy laughed, partly in surprise, partly in amusement. "This isn't like you! You're behaving like your sister!" Then she sobered up a little. "Are you sure about this? Don't get me wrong; I like the boy. My spirit takes him. But are you *sure?*"

I said, "If I never see him again, it would be worth it."

Like a bad taste in my mouth, I remembered the first time I slept with Storm—me and my ninety-day-rule in action. I'd waited three months with Storm, and he still turned out to be a madman who could have cost me my life. So if waiting longer didn't assure my safety, why the hell not?

And with that I spruced up and jaunted off. It was after ten, and I texted him to say I was on the way. At 10:31 p.m., as I was sliding the keycard into the lock, I got another text: "Hello?"

A little eager, were we?

He took it slow, like a gentleman. We talked for a long time … but not too long. The night was slipping away, and we were eager to explore each other. We brushed our teeth together and showered together. He soaped my back. Hotel soap never smelled so good.

He put out a spread of nibbles and wine, and we ate and talked some more. I wanted to make sure he knew where I was coming from, so I told him, straight up, "Understand this: I made a conscious decision to come here. If I never see you again, no bad blood, no recriminations. I'd be okay."

"I don't think that's going to be the case," he replied at once. "Just letting you know."

Then we had mind-blowing sex. It was un-freaking-real. This man was a different kind of lover. He worshipped me from head to toe, removed my shoes, unzipped me ... It was all about me.

I'd planned to stay only a few hours, but every time I tried to leave, he gave me several excellent reasons to stay. At one point we were lying together, just holding each other, not talking, knowing we had to get up to hit the shower but reluctant to break the embrace.

From out of nowhere, he whispered, "I know ... I know. We'll work it out."

I lifted my head to look at him, puzzled. "I haven't said anything."

"You didn't have to. We'll work it out. Don't worry."

It was mystifying, but comforting, that he was able to pick up on my thoughts and anxieties without me even having to speak them out loud. The question was, did I really want a man, even a man this good, living in my head?

By seven in the morning, the spirit might have been willing but the flesh was worn out, and so we tumbled out of bed and took another shower, which, believe me, we both needed. He performed last night's ritual of undressing me, only in reverse, helping me into my clothes and buckling my shoes, raising the bar for every other man I ever had.

"Any regrets?" he asked as we left. I had none.

He made it just in time to check in for his flight and decided to while away his time in the lounge by sending me a series of dirty—and immensely enjoyable—texts. The digital conversation continued through the flight, and he let me know when he had landed and was on his way home.

That set the precedent for the way things were to continue—an ongoing back-and-forth of messages, from the intimate to the mundane, that have kept us connected across the distance. I became spoiled by them, looking forward to my daily dose of "Good morning, sweetheart; hope you have a lovely day. Thinking about you." Because really, what woman wouldn't?

Months after what should have been a one-night stand, Aamir and I were still in daily contact. I had a conference in Costa Rica, two months after we met, and he convinced me to delay my layover and instead spend the weekend with him. My decision? Well, obviously, I said yes.

He ramped up the anticipation by starting a countdown, texting me every morning with "Five more days, lover ... four more ..." It was long-distance foreplay and I was loving it. I went ziplining in Costa Rica, and he warned me to be careful. "I'm looking forward to seeing you! Don't let anything happen to you!"

He picked me up at the airport with a hug and a kiss. He was like an excited little boy. "You made it! You made it!"

I was melting in the heat, frantically fanning, so he ushered me into the car, saying, "I have a bottle of water and an apple on the seat for you. Go; I'll get your luggage."

We talked throughout the hour-and-a-half drive to his home. He cleared me a space to set up my technology, and when I was done, I turned to face him. He was standing there smiling, with his arms open wide. I walked into his arms, and he said, "Let's go take a shower." Exactly what I wanted to hear.

I hadn't told anyone where I was going, partly because this was new and different, and partly because I enjoyed the excitement of a secret rendezvous with this gorgeous man. But it seems I raised my daughter to be one smart cookie, because she called me soon after I fell off the radar, laughing. "I know you so well. You went to Aamir's, didn't you?"

It's hard to get caught out in in a clandestine booty call by your own girl-child, so I played innocent. "Why do you say that?"

"Because," said Miss Smartypants, "you're supposed to be on a plane, but you're answering your phone. Now put that man on the phone!"

I handed over the phone and watched as my daughter put some schooling into him. He pressed the phone to his ear, caressing the inside of my wrist with his free hand, with the biggest grin on his face, and all I could hear was him saying, over and over, "Yes ma'am. Yes ma'am." I burned so badly to know what the conversation was about that I could have screamed.

He passed the phone to me and dictated his address and his mother's name so I could text them to my daughter. I was mystified, but did as I was told. Moments later, my daughter called back. "Put Aamir on again," she ordered. I handed it over, feeling as if these two were planning a party and I wasn't invited.

"You have a beautiful home," I heard her tell him. It turned out she'd plugged his address into Google Earth and done some amateur surveillance.

Aamir was as impressed as I was. "I now officially worship the ground your daughter walks on," he said. "I hope my daughters grow up to be like that." I explained that she and I had been on our own for a long time, so we'd become extremely close.

And after the nasty shocks I'd had when Storm's filthy past was eventually revealed, I'd also decided to do a little digging into Aamir's files, albeit a little late. Since I'd already slept with him— repeatedly and with great enthusiasm—I'd say the horse of caution had already bolted. But I guess you could say that the information became important when I realized that our little adventure was turning out to be more than a one-night stand. It's easier online than you think. *Tap-tap-tap* and damning evidence, such as police files, are there on your screen. Fortunately he came up clean.

Anyway, that weekend we were inseparable. He was an expert at long-distance relationships, it seems. When he and his ex-wife were dating, they lived in separate states and went to visit each other in alternate months. When they were together, he told me, they wouldn't come up for air.

Oho, I thought. *Let's see how this weekend is going to compare.*

Well, I'm pleased to report that he not only met but also exceeded all my expectations. He wooed me with music and wine; it was the first time I'd ever heard the Kem song "Promise to Love." The lyrics were so stirring, and touched us so deeply, that we actually stopped in the middle of our lovemaking to listen. It was about looking for love, almost losing hope, and then, from out of nowhere, finding it. It touched us both in a profound, personal way. I'd always thought Kem was for young people, but that night he sang for both of us.

And when the song was over, you guessed it, we returned to our regularly scheduled programming—namely copious amounts of amazing sex. The next morning, I spotted a neighbor staring across the way at me with her huge, round eyes, making no secret of the fact that she was curious about my appearance. I don't blame her; Aamir is a noisy one. Let's just say his neighbors now know my name. In fact, I'm surprised they didn't call the police.

I teased him about it, but he protested, "But that's what you do to me!" It's not bad to be in your fifties and still capable of making a man howl like a wolf in the moonlight!

Before I'd arrived, I'd made the world's most unromantic request. I'd been trying to shake a nagging chest cough, and my doctor had asked if I snored. Since when I'm at home the only two people in my bed were me and my shadow, I hadn't been able to answer that question, so when I got to Aamir's I asked him to observe overnight and report in the morning. Then came the sex, and I forgot about it. He didn't.

The next morning, he delivered his review. "You don't snore, by the way. You sleep in one spot, and you breathe very softly. I almost had to listen to hear if you were breathing." That, I think, was a much more fun way to get the information I needed than setting up a recorder!

"What do you want to do for breakfast?" he asked.

"I'm not a breakfast person," I said; never mind that we'd collectively expended a thousand calories the night before.

"That's okay. I want to take you out to lunch, and then we can go to the movies." Wow. Ten points! We went window shopping, had lunch, saw a movie, and returned to his cave for a second helping of the sexual feast we'd enjoyed the night before.

The next morning, he went in to work and left me alone in his house for a couple of hours. To me, this is a different type of intimacy. Two people who are in sync with each other can have good sex, but to give a virtual stranger free run of your home, unsupervised, is a declaration of trust that I appreciate and will endeavor to live up to.

While I was sitting around being impressed, he came back and ramped it up yet another level by offering to do my laundry so I would be returning home with clean clothes instead of a dank pile of postvacation rubble that would send me to the laundry for hours. Who was I to say no?

Much of it was underwear, including the purpose-bought Victoria's Secret negligee sets I'd worn for him on Friday and Saturday night. Without batting an eyelid, he washed all my stuff together with his. Significant, yes? Because washing underwear together is a whole lot more intimate than, say, having a laugh over a sizzling steak—or even the kind of sex we'd been enjoying all weekend. Who'd have thought that the laundry room would have become the great meeting place of our souls?

With everything cleaned and dried, I began wrestling all the loot from the previous day's shopping spree into my unwilling suitcase. It was like trying to cram five pounds of oranges into a tube sock; it just wasn't going to happen—at least, not until Aamir came to the rescue.

"I'm an expert packer. If you have nothing to hide in your suitcase, I'd be happy to make sure everything fits," he offered.

I assured him that I had no contraband, blood diamonds, or sex toys hidden away among my blouses and pajamas, so he had a go. Miracle of miracles, it worked. *What a man*, I thought. *Good in bed, knows how to choose a wine, gives foot massages,* and *can pack a suitcase? He's a keeper.*

Monday came, and the last wisps of our dream weekend began to dissipate. It was time for him to go to work, and for me to fly home. Side by side we stood, brushing our teeth, as had become our habit. Our eyes caught in the mirror. We had the same thought. "It feels like we've known each other forever, doesn't it?" he told me. I was glad he voiced it, because I was almost afraid to.

We both acknowledge that there is something there; we just don't know exactly what it is.

A ONE-NIGHT-STAND
TURNS INTO MORE

That was in June. The next time I saw Aamir was in August. I flew in from London, and he'd brought his daughters back to their home and was babysitting them for the weekend. I had been incommunicado while in London because my phone never connected, but I determined I would let him know before I left that I was headed there. Once I landed, I sent him a text, and he responded that he was also in town. I asked whether I could see him, and he called immediately.

To my surprise, his first question was "So who'd you go to London with?" This was very quietly asked and deceptively casual.

"My daughter, Mummy, and my niece" was my immediate response.

"I'll be there in an hour," he said.

Notwithstanding our relationship, I felt it necessary to ask my daughter's permission to entertain him. Of course she agreed, and she left the house to give us some privacy. When he arrived and I opened the door, he hugged me for what seemed an eternity—no words, just a bear hug. We talked for a bit—just a bit—and then ...

He didn't disappoint me. And based on his reaction, I guess I didn't disappoint him, either. He left after a few hours, having to make the one-hour drive back to pick up his girls from the nail salon.

Once his girls were settled, he called me, and we chatted for a bit. He asked whether he could see me the next day. I agreed, so he booked me into a hotel just around the corner from the house so we could be close, without me intruding on their family time. His children live in his marital home with his ex-wife, and she was going out of town, so he had agreed babysit.

I settled in at the hotel, and he'd pop over from time to time to pay me a visit. Between dropping off his girls and picking them up, he and I would get chunks of hours together. It was here that I got to know more about his past and delve deeper into who he really was. I asked; he talked. He asked; I talked.

I admit, though, that there's a deep spiritual connection between me and Aamir; that much was obvious from the first time we spoke. But I will not let it manifest into something I am not prepared to be part of. I will not get married again. I'd rather do the Tina Turner intercontinental relationship thing, with him happy where he is and me happy wherever I am in the world, the two of us getting together to enjoy each other whenever we can. I'm comfy with that.

I'd even say the time apart sharpens our desire for each other and our appreciation for time spent together. When we do get together, we don't want to waste our precious few days together on trivialities.

Aamir's touch is different from Storm's. For some reason, a deeply guarded part of his soul has opened to me, and neither of us fully understands why. This was supposed to be a one-night stand, and look at us now. It's probably because it was *supposed* to be a one-night stand that we felt free to be so unguarded and open, without any boundaries. It was the purest kind of sexual energy, especially for me, because I figured I'd never see him again.

He's a man who isn't afraid to admit when he's wrong. He's good at taking responsibility for his actions. He's such a nice person; it's difficult to stay mad at him. He has a quiet strength about him, like a gentle giant. And his work ethic is above reproach, whereas Storm refused to even work.

And as much as we enjoy what we have, and as eager as we are to discover what's going to come, I made sure to draw the line with him, if only for my own protection. "I'm my own woman," I told him, "and I will always be. Don't sweat me. Don't blow up my phone. If you call me and can't reach me, don't ask me where I went. Don't ask me when I will be back. I've been through hell and came out the other side. I'm not going there again."

"Why did the girls put you on the dating website?" he asked.

"My life is complicated," I explained. "I'm not going to find anyone under normal circumstances. First, I'm too picky ..." I guess he can take that as a compliment. "And second, I never know if my foot is on this continent or that one. I'm always traveling. I can't ask a man to be involved with me knowing he won't see me often. And I demand fidelity. And that's just not fair to a man."

"I don't have a problem with that," he said—a simple but essential response.

I have to confess now that I chickened out. I pretended not to hear his answer, because there was so much tied up in that one response that it was nearly impossible for me to untangle and unpack it all at once. So I stayed silent.

"WE'LL FIGURE THIS OUT"

Even though Aamir is a professional, I'm not sure this relationship isn't still a case of dating down. Sometimes my mind wanders back to the issue of being evenly yoked. I wonder whether I should let the absence of pedigree be an issue.

Yes, yes, I understand that he's a qualified professional, but he's a simple soul. He's married to his job, but he's not a social climber. I see more of his grandparents in him than his mom. He spent significantly more time with them than he ever did with her, and he inherited their simplicity and frugality. Although he lives well, he is still a bargain shopper. Yet he's open and generous with his money, not at all cheap.

There's an element to this that I appreciate and even admire. He once discovered a small parson's table that someone had thrown out, and he rescued it, sanded it down, varnished it, and presented it to his mother with love. Other people may find this embarrassing, but he told me about it with pride.

But I justify my little prejudice by saying that I'm not looking for another husband. I live a complicated life, and I'm not about to link myself with someone who might cause me to stagnate.

Furthermore, what does dating up mean? What is dating on the same level? I dated a man who was both white and a doctor, and it turned out he'd raped one of his nurses. So what does dating up mean?

Setting aside the question of up, down, and sideways for a while, I've eliminated many types of men from my dating pool: Trinis, West Indians, Africans, and Haitians. I also don't date Jamaicans; they're too brash, and I've gotten enough horn to last me a lifetime. He'd have to come really well! That notwithstanding, everyone has an opportunity to impress me.

It's a tough bill to fill, made even more complicated by the fact that a lot of men on my level—educated professionals—don't seem to want women like me. Instead they seek out younger, less educated, less accomplished women, thus making themselves seem smarter, richer, and better by comparison. It's a control thing; they enjoy having women look up to them.

I also think they like younger women because men are very visual and their image of desirability, whether media-induced or not, is almost always that of someone young and fresh-faced. This is not so with Aamir, though, at least as far as I'm concerned. Although I'm older than he is by three years, he often says, only half-joking, "You're wearing this brother out."

He insists I'm younger than I say I am, even going so far as checking my driver's license in his quest for proof of age. "Are you *sure?*" he asks me. I take that as a compliment. I do give him a run for his money in bed, though, because trust me, I'm well versed.

I hated having oral sex with Storm; it felt one-sided, even degrading. It was as if I only gave of myself, and he only took and consumed. But with Aamir it is different. I love doing it for him: I love the reaction I can draw from him, and he, in turn, loves mine. It is fully reciprocal, fully give-and-take, as sex with Aamir always is.

This man can't decide which fascinates him more, my brain or my body, and I have given him full access to both. This fascination is why, even though we seldom inhabit the same space, our interaction is so intense when we do get together. That mental connection fuels our slowly bubbling chemistry so that when we meet, our connection is volatile and deep.

My most recent publication—prior to this gem you're holding, that is—was a chapter in an academic book. I sent him a copy. I hadn't thought it possible for our interaction to become more profound than it already was, but after he read my writing, it did. He thereafter had a deeper level of admiration for me, along with respect for my intellect and who I am as a professional. He likes the way I speak, and as he once said, "But more than that, I like the way your mind works."

And yet I sense some fear in him. Despite his professional qualifications and experience, he asks himself why I am with him. He's having a hard time shaking the idea that *I* am dating down.

He's cautious—maybe even overly cautious. I try not to be impatient; I get it. He's been hurt badly by that bitch he married. I also think he's progressing carefully out of respect and concern for me, wanting to demonstrate how much he values me while also letting me know that what was supposed to be a booty call has gone beyond that.

In a contradictory way, our mutual belief that the thing between us was just temporary worked in our favor. It encouraged, rather than hampered, our bonding. It allowed him and me to start off with complete honesty, perhaps because we felt there was nothing at stake—nothing to be gained by saying the "right" things or pretending to be someone we're not.

It set a different tone for every interaction—every conversation. We talk about sex like two men: with no embarrassment. Yet it's not obscene or uncomfortable; it's just frank and unashamed. I asked him, "How did you learn to be such a mind-blowing lover?"

He showed me his collection of erotic how-tos: the *Kama Sutra* and other sex manuals. He studies women's bodies. It amazes me that a man who is so elementally sexual, who spent his marriage being denied that simple interaction, still refused to be unfaithful to his wife. I think, *Here I am bitching about living with Satan for three years, and Aamir stayed in a loveless marriage for over twenty without becoming bitter.* I can tell that his marriage changed him. I can see the difference in photos between the man he was years ago, glowing and happy, with an open expression, and the guarded, more sober man he is today.

By comparison, I feel as if I dodged a bullet. Although if I were honest, I'd admit that that bullet went clean through me and came out the other side.

It's not as important to me that others should find me desirable as much as it is that I should like what I see in the mirror. I don't care that much about what other people think. If I like what I see, I'm good.

I do like to feel desired by the man who matters to me. It's important that he finds me physically attractive, even though Aamir isn't much into appearances. The Victoria's Secret trousseau I wore the last time I visited might just as well have been flannel jammies and bunny slippers for all the attention he paid them. But he tells me all the time that I, for myself, am attractive to him, and I like that. He openly lets me know that he thinks I'm sexy.

POSTPONED LASAGNA
AND SHARED LAUNDRY

My monthlong trip was one of those hectic jaunts that saw me bouncing back and forth across the Atlantic. I flew to London on New Year's Eve and spent ten days there. I did some clubbing, of course, and hung out with my cousins. And of course you can't beat the shopping there.

After my sessions in London ended, I flew to the United States, where I got to see my sister for a few days, and then spent some time with my daughter.

And then came my week with Aamir. How was it? Let me put it this way: I have a friend who says that every time I talk about him, I get a hot flash. "I've been paying attention," she said to me. "Whenever his name comes up, you pull out your fan and start fanning yourself." Talk about having a tell! It would probably be a bad idea for me to play poker with him in the room.

Before this visit, we'd only done weekends and sneaked a day in here or then when our schedules allowed, so this time was different enough for me to be hovering somewhere between excitement and uncertainty. I needn't have worried; each time we've gotten together has been better than the time before.

I flew nonstop from London, and he came to pick me up in his backup car. It turned out that he was giving it a stretch on the road so it would be warmed up for me to use during the week I was there.

The moment we stepped inside his house, he placed the car keys and a set of house keys into the palm of my hand and taught me the code for his alarm system. I don't need to expand on what an honor it was for a man I knew intimately, but not for very long, to confer that level of trust on me.

Of course, sex was on both our minds, and who can blame us? We hadn't seen each other in five months. But I'd been traveling for a long time, so he tried to be a gentleman, God bless him. "I suppose you must be exhausted," he ventured.

"Not *that* exhausted!" I countered, and we both laughed.

That first morning, he made sure I was settled, kissed me good-bye, and left me to my work. I was working on several things at the same time, as usual: publications, proposals, and a chapter of my latest book. He popped back in at lunchtime, eager to see me. I was dressing to go to the grocery, but of course that little expedition got delayed.

As I've said before, I don't cook. Don't ask; I just don't. But for Aamir, I decided to make an exception. Naturally, I needed a spirit guide, and mine came in the form of my sister, who is a master chef. I called her up and explained I had two menus in mind: turkey lasagna on Wednesday and baked sweet potatoes with cinnamon and brown sugar and baked salmon on Thursday. She dictated my shopping list, and off I went.

I came back weighed down with groceries and began putting things away, excited about the experiment that was to come. I spread out the ingredients for the lasagna, browned the turkey—and realized I'd forgotten the marinara sauce. Great start.

Resourceful woman that I am, I didn't panic. The salmon was already seasoned, so I put away the lasagna fixings and popped the sweet potatoes into the oven, along with the salmon.

Ever courteous, Aamir called to tell me he was stuck in a meeting and would be a little late, which gave me a little more time. When he got home, he set the table, he served dinner, and we talked. It was warm, domestic, and completely without the artifice that always seems to pervade the early part of a relationship.

I made sure he understood what an effort it was for me to put on an apron and pick up a spatula. "I literally cook for no one," I told him. "I. Do. Not. Cook."

"That's why they're all laughing at you!" he said.

"Yup. That's why."

After dinner, we were still talking about each other's days. He motioned me not to get up. "I'll do the dishes," he said, which was fine with me.

Of course, my daughter isn't the kind of woman to let anything slide, so it wasn't long before the phone started ringing. "How was the food?" she asked. My whole family was fully apprised of my quest into untested culinary territory, and they were so curious as to how it went that they were getting hives.

"It was good," I told her, but she wasn't buying it.

"I don't believe you," she said. "You can't cook." If I didn't love that child so much, I'd have felt insulted.

Aamir nobly took the phone and spoke up for me. "It was," he insisted. "It was really good!" This news eventually made it into the family WhatsApp chat group, a clear indication of (1) how bad my reputation as a non-cook really is and (2) how my relatives have nothing better to do with their time.

After dinner, I retreated into the bedroom while he relaxed in the living room—not that I didn't want to spend time with him, but I know he's a loner at heart, and I wanted to give him some space. I heard him talking to his daughters on the phone and heard the hum of the TV. After an hour, he came in. "Aren't you coming to watch TV with me?"

Pleased by the invitation, I followed him out, and we curled up on the sofa. He got me a blanket and wrapped it around me, probably thinking I was asleep. But I wasn't; to paraphrase Aerosmith, I didn't want to fall asleep 'cause I didn't want to miss a thing.

The next day followed the same pattern. He left for work and came back just to have lunch with me. Now, the way Aamir's house is set up, one can come down the hall toward the bedroom and see what's going on in the bathroom reflected in the bedroom mirror. It's not exactly discreet—especially if you're like me and enjoy dancing alone in the bathroom in Victoria's Secret lingerie.

I had my headphones on, enjoying the groove—you know how I love to dance—and didn't realize that he was just standing there, getting an eyeful.

When he eventually made his presence known, he did so with a tinge of regret. "I should have stood there and watched you dance a little longer," he teased. Apparently he could also hear me singing from the outside of the house!

Apart from the vicarious pleasure it gave him, he said he was also glad to see me so relaxed in his home.

The next day, I drove back to the grocery to pick up the marinara sauce I'd forgotten the day before, and I made him the promised lasagna. And no, it didn't suck.

On Friday, I took him to a special spa I'd been planning to visit. It was going to be a surprise for more than one reason, and when he arrived, he assumed we'd be having something fairly tame, like a couples massage. He was wrong.

This particular spa had a flotation tank—the kind where you immerse yourself in 10 inches of body-warm water in which eight hundred to one thousand pounds of Epsom salts have been dissolved. Isolated, and with other stimuli, such as light and sound, removed, you experience a level of introspective peace and calm that is almost womb-like.

I enjoyed the look of incredulity on Aamir's face as the therapist explained the procedure. "Really?" he asked.

"Really," I responded, almost gloating when I thought of how soon his skepticism would turn to pleasure.

Floating, as it is called, is a solitary affair, so we parted and stripped naked in our individual chambers. We showered and stepped in, and then for the next hour that tiny space was our universe. When it was over, his doubt had been replaced by a glowing new wonder. It was awkward at first, he told me, but then he got into it. The next thing he knew, he was awakened an hour later by the gurgle of the piping, having completely succumbed to the lull of that amniotic immersion.

I was glad that he was able to relax, especially since he was normally so tense and tired. I myself had been sore after such a hectic few weeks, but when I emerged, I was fine. He kissed me and thanked me for the experience, just as he always thanked me for dinner.

He took me to see his office; he plays it down a lot, but he has quite a lot of influence. His office complex is huge, and he is an integral part of the current expansion, which is why he's been so busy lately. It's complicated, detailed work that will probably go on for another six months, but when he's done, he plans to do some traveling with me—not for a week, but for a considerable chunk of time. I guess that means I'd better expand my culinary expertise to include a few more recipes!

As Aamir showed me around, his pride and love for his job showed on his face. "You must really love your job," I observed.

"I do," he responded simply. That's why working seven days a week is his norm and why he has no problem with it. While there are opportunities for promotion, he lets them go by because he is so passionate about what he is doing now. "I am where I'm supposed to be," he says. Not many people can say that, and it's just one more reason I like him so much.

His job was such that we didn't have much time to be together, but that didn't worry me. I didn't feel neglected in any way. As a matter of fact, many times I was so busy I hardly had time for him. One day he came home for lunch and I was on a conference call and couldn't get away. He kissed me on the forehead, had his lunch, and slipped out quietly—no bother, no fuss. I like this about him and about our situation. His lack of jealousy shows me how mature and selfless he is. It's also proof that we recognize that each of us is a full-fledged, independent entity with a job to do and a life to live. And our comfort around each other at his home was almost domestic; we did each other's laundry, and while he was away I tidied up. In my mind, I have the image of myself shaking together a portion of sugar and another of flour until they are well blended. We lived like husband and wife, but there was no pressure.

It was a relaxed little bubble that we made all our own, yet we never allowed fantasy to erode our understanding of the impermanence of that week. That, I guess, is what you call being truly grown up.

A big part of being grown up, I think, is learning that love translates into different things for different people. We did the Five Love Languages test. I was curious to see what our results would be. It's quite a popular test, but in the event that you aren't aware of it, it simply states that people receive and express love in five major ways: words of affirmation, acts of service, gifts, quality time, and physical touch. It comes with a short questionnaire, and one afternoon we administered the test to each other.

Unsurprisingly, his profile came up with physical touch, followed by words of affirmation. In turn, my profile reflected a desire for quality time first, followed by words of affirmation. I guess this explains why I so much appreciated his allowing me into his personal space, and the effort he made to be with me even though he is swamped by such a demanding job.

When the week ended, he took me back to the airport. This time our parting was different. On my last visit, our farewell hug was sustained—the kind where you break apart and hold on to each other again and again. It was the embarrassing kind, when you're sure people are watching. I almost cried.

This time he disappeared quickly, almost as if he didn't want me to see his face as I left, or to experience that pulling sensation in his chest. He kissed me, handed over my luggage, and was out of there.
No "I love you"

You're probably dying to ask, but so far, we have not said "I love you" to each other. But that's okay. It's not something I need to hear. Once, during sex, Aamir blurted out, "This is how you deserve to be loved, and I will always love you this way," but I'm not putting much stock in that as an indicator. After all, some people talk during sex, and he's one of them.

He has progressed from calling me "sweetheart" and "love" to calling me "baby", but I pretend I don't hear it. I won't consider us to be in a relationship until and unless we specifically define it as such. I may sound funny, but that's who I am.

I did tell him, however, that I am monogamous, so the fact that I am sleeping with him means I'm not sleeping with anyone else. We even discussed testing for STDs, from the first time, and ensured our use of protection. In a way, I see that as a level of commitment—or, at least, sanity. And the sex? It's much more intimate and intense now. And I'll take that, thanks.

I even asked, in wonder, why his ex-wife had ever given him up. "She never loved me," he replied, almost casually, as if it didn't hurt anymore.

One thing that adds to the surprising level of comfort between us is our lack of bitterness toward our spouses from hell. I see none in him, and he sees none in me. We've come to each other with clean slates, and that has made all the difference.

But I am aware that this thing is just for a season; Aamir is not "the one". He's a sweet man, but he's just not strong enough for me. But I have also made up my mind that I will enjoy every last second of this season. I'm the strength of my family, and I require strength in return. I need a mountain.

And yet his strength seems to be in his quietness and in the peaceful space he creates for me to escape to. Hmm ... maybe he's not as weak as I think. Maybe my concept of strength has always been flawed.

HOW STAR TREK
COULD SAVE US

I t frustrates me when people make decisions based on how they
feel about another person, especially in the professional arena.
Work and sentiment have nothing to do with each other. But the
problem is that we favor the people we like. If we can't overcome
that to move toward a common goal, then we have lost sight of what
is important.

Of course, I'm not throwing shade, but with my fresher
perspective, I can see the sense of entitlement so many have. Why
can't we commit to the longevity of anything, especially in this
time and space? Why do we need instant gratification? And that's
a worldwide problem. Yet we have a low level of commitment to
anything. It seems to me we've lost two generations: parents who
don't know how to parent, and children making children. sometimes
I'm so frustrated I feel as if I'm going to implode.

I think that being on a judge's bench would be a way to educate
people. Punishment doesn't have to be truly punitive as long as the
person learns the lesson he or she was meant to learn. Judges who
sentence slumlords to live in their own buildings? I love that kind
of stuff! Paying a fine means nothing to people like that; they're
millionaires. But sentence them to live six months in their own

cockroach-infested building? Yeah, that's justice. That's what I'd like to do.

Failing that, I think I'll just become a Star Trek captain. I'm a serious Trekkie. I'm a sci-fi fanatic. My absolute favorite is *Star Trek: Discovery* and I am absolutely love Captain Michael Burnham.

There are deeper messages about life in these shows—powerful messages that are so different from how we view things in this society.

And the men on these shows are well worth watching. Tyr Anasazi, anybody? He's that gorgeous dreadlocked Nietzschean mercenary in Andromeda. If you don't know who he is, go ahead and Google him. I'll wait ...

You're welcome.

The End

It's now been more than a year and a half since Aamir and I met; in fact, on the anniversary of our meeting, he made the comment, almost to himself, that he should have gotten me a card. I was so stunned that I had no comeback, so I let it slide without responding.

A few months later, we arranged to meet when he traveled to his cousin's wedding. As usual, we spent a wonderful night together, showered together, and brushed our teeth together. And in the morning, he sneaked out to move my car from the front to the side of the hotel. I had the niggling feeling that he was doing so because he was didn't want his family to know about me, especially when we took the back way out to the car. But once we got to the car, he was his usual demonstrative self, kissing me at every opportunity. So what if he felt it was inappropriate for his family, including his mother, to see us together? I still don't know if his mother knows about me, as I have never met her or his daughters. This may seem strange, but it doesn't bother me. Remember: it started off as a casual thing, a chance meeting online, before it began growing into this unidentified "something other." So maybe he needs to determine what exactly "this" is before he brings his family on board.

The wedding seems to have been another watershed moment for us. We were inseparable, and he was late picking up the groom the next morning. He kept saying we had to get up but never actually made a move to do so. I did notice, though, that there was more affection between us than usual. The passion was at its usual level— it gets better every time, it seems—but we hugged more and kissed more.

He was also more attentive. I showed up with a new haircut, and he couldn't keep his fingers out of it. He kept making me spin around, turning from side to side, to admire me. He loved what I was wearing, right down to my shoes. He set up a workstation next to my bed, with extra outlets for my devices. He couldn't even step out of the shower without kissing me good-bye. He treated me like royalty.

After the wedding, we parted company, going back to our busy separate lives. He set up my Waze so I could find my way back, and he asked when he would see me again. "My schedule is packed," I told him, "so it may not be possible for a while. Unless you're ready to come to travel with me."

"I'm not ready yet," he replied, "but soon, I will be."

That parting was hard. He got up, walked away, returned to kiss me again, and came back yet another time to sit in the car until he was sure I was ready to leave—or maybe it was until he could muster up the strength to leave.

Over the second half of the year, I was hardly on the ground, traveling from the United States to the UK, Europe, and Africa. To his credit, he doesn't have a problem with my wanderlust; he even seems intrigued by it. He often jokes when I call him, asking, "Where in the world are you now?" as though I'm Carmen Sandiego.

He pumps me for details about my trips, what I've seen and where I'm going next. He now asks about my job, trying to understand how I define myself professionally.

Our deepening relationship—if we have the courage to call it that—has been like peeling back the layers of an onion. Even the music he plays for me has changed. That first year, I remember him playing a raunchy rap booty call song. The last time I saw him, when we got together on my birthday, the song he played—giving me specific instructions to listen carefully—was about a man coming to terms with his feelings for a woman. It was a beautiful song. I'd never heard the artist before; we listened to the entire album on our ride home from the airport, and at one point we were singing and humming the catchy chorus together. It just seemed so comfortable. We were so in tune.

When we arrived at the house for my birthday visit, Aamir walked past me into the bathroom and asked over his shoulder, "Could you bring me a bottle of water, please?"

This was an unusual request, to be sure, but I quickly hopped up and went to the kitchen, only to see an exquisitely decorated birthday cake on the counter. I turned around, and he was standing there, smiling. "You didn't even question my request to bring me water," he said in wonderment.

"What's the big deal?" I said. "You're always getting things for me!"

Next to the cake was a birthday card that said how loving and kind I'd been to him, and that I had planted a seed in his heart. It said, "Happy Birthday, sweetheart," and was signed "'Mir."

I think one of the more important elements of our relationship is not the sex or the physical affection, but the fact that I care about Aamir's health and well-being. I send him supplements and vitamins to make sure he's up on his dietary requirements. Not many people do that for him, I gather, and that's rather sad.

In some ways, we act like an old married couple when we're together. He calls me to let me know when he will be late from the office, and he eats what I cook, even though I'm certainly not the world's best chef. I call to check on him when I sense something isn't going well, and most times, I'm right. When you get to know someone so deeply, your sixth sense kicks in.

We talked a lot on that visit; he even said that he thought I was falling in love with him. I wasn't going to give him the victory so easily. "What gives you that idea?" I asked.

He looked smug. "I can't tell you all my secrets, but let's just say it's based on the things you do."

"How long have you believed that?"

"For quite a while."

Oh really? "Assuming it's true," I hedged, "does it bother you?"

"I'm still here, aren't I?"

Of course, I'm still undecided about whether I'm ready to give this thing between us a name, but as Aamir said, regardless of how much we are or aren't willing to admit, we can't deny our deep attraction to one another.

And at that, we let it go.

Since then we've been trying to meet up whenever we can. Transatlantic relationships are never easy, especially when I'm scooting all around the world for work, seminars, and just to take a little side trip with my daughter or to visit friends.

So I'm looking forward to seeing how this thing between me and Aamir plays out, with a mixture of curiosity and excitement. It has the potential to become something wonderful, as long as the goalposts don't shift. I won't stop traveling; I intend to continue living my life on my terms and advancing my career as I see fit.

He's said he's okay with it, so I don't expect him to start making demands. As they say, if it ain't broke, don't fix it. And at the moment, it's working.

So my present is great; I'm exactly where I want to be. And I'm not scared about my future; I have no worry, no apprehension—and I have to thank my ex-husband, Storm, for that, because if I can survive what he put me through, I can survive anything.

Printed in the United States
by Baker & Taylor Publisher Services